TEXAS MEN

TEXAS MEN

PAUL EVAN LEHMAN

M. EVANS
Lanham • Boulder • New York • Toronto • Plymouth, UK

Published by M. Evans
An imprint of Rowman & Littlefield
4501 Forbes Boulevard, Suite 200, Lanham, Maryland 20706
www.rowman.com

10 Thornbury Road, Plymouth PL6 7PP, United Kingdom

Distributed by National Book Network

British Library Cataloguing in Publication Information Available

Library of Congress Cataloging-in-Publication Data

Library of Congress Control Number: 2014907794

ISBN: 978-1-59077-422-9 (pbk. : alk. paper)
ISBN: 978-1-59077-423-6 (electronic)

♾™ The paper used in this publication meets the minimum requirements of
American National Standard for Information Sciences—Permanence of
Paper for Printed Library Materials, ANSI/NISO Z39.48-1992.

Printed in the United States of America

TO

MY WIFE

CONTENTS

CHAPTER I

THE RAID

Two men crouched at the edge of the cliff gazing into the valley below. Behind them, in a clump of bushes, stood their horses; farther beyond, a dozen hard-faced, unkempt riders lounged in their saddles, talking gruffly.

In the valley, three wagons were drawn up near a spring, and a cooking fire crackled cheerfully. Beyond, on the flats, several hundred head of cattle, having been watered, were being bunched by six weary cowpunchers.

One of the kneeling men, a shaggy-browed, black-bearded giant, spoke to his companion. "Nice bunch of beef, Shab. A little trail ga'nted, but they will fatten up fine. Only seven men, not countin' the cook and the kid."

His companion grunted. "That ain't no kid; that's a girl."

Kurt Dodd thrust his big head forward and squinted against the dying sun. "Danged if you ain't right! Must be Tomlinson's daughter. Well, it makes no difference. I'm danged glad Bob Lee and his outfit ain't located them yet. Duke Haslam sent word that they rode out of Lariat aimin' to help Tomlinson with the drive. They're salty gents, and might make it hot for us."

"Who's with Lee?"

"The bunch that rode for him before he sold out to Tomlinson: Ace Talbot, Deuce Lowery, that Mexican of his, and Dick."

The other grunted again and shifted his position. He was squat and powerful, with a shock of red hair and numerous freckles. His rough garb was that of the range, and included a once ornate but now disreputable calfskin vest. "Reckon you can count on Dick keepin' 'em out of our way?"

"Duke's been talkin' to him," Dodd answered cryptically. "Well, Tomlinson is goin' to bed down here. We might as well pull out."

He inched away from the edge of the cliff, got to his feet, and strode to his waiting horse. The man called Shab followed. They mounted and joined their men. The little group had stiffened expectantly.

"Like takin' candy from a kid," Kurt Dodd told them shortly. "Come dark we'll circle and strike on the west side. Stampede the cows into those gullies over here. Let's go."

The men turned their horses. It was an old story to them. A swift dash through the night, flaming guns, the thunder of hoofs; then when the animals had run the fright out of their systems, the hurried cutting out of the likeliest ones and the drive by devious trails into the hills. To them cattle rustling was a business and they went about it in a businesslike way.

Some two miles north of the valley's head, bacon sizzled and coffee gurgled over another camp fire. About it were gathered four men, cowmen by their attire. Three were Americans: Ace Talbot, six feet five; Deuce Lowery, five feet six; Bob Lee, half way between. The fourth was a Mexican of average height, lithe as a cougar, almost effeminate in his languid appearance. Bob Lee was sitting on his heels poking at the bacon; the other three sprawled on the ground amiably quarreling.

"It's about time we was meetin' up with Tomlinson," said Deuce. "First thing you know we'll be clear down in Texas."

"You won't," drawled Ace. "Not with that sheriff waitin' for you."

"He's waitin' for you, too. It was yore fault to begin with. If you hadn't horned into my private war and started bustin' mirrors and bottles we wouldn't 'a' had to leave by the window head first."

"Yeah, and if I hadn't horned in you'd 'a' left by the door feet first."

"*Señores!*" protested José Villegas. "No quarrel, pliz. I'm theenk of new song I'm hear in Santone. Eef I had my guitar I would play heem."

Bob Lee got up quickly and raised a hand for silence. The snap of breaking brush, the thud of hoofs came to them, and a moment later a horseman rode up and dropped from the saddle.

Bob addressed him. "Any sign of Tomlinson, Dick?"

Dick Markley answered without looking up. "No. Didn't go far; just to the head of the valley." He slipped the bridle and dragged the saddle from his horse's back. Ropes stretched from tree to tree formed a rude corral, and into this he drove the animal. Presently he joined them at the fire and proceeded to roll a cigarette. As yet he had not looked directly at Bob or his companions.

A handsome young man was Dick Markley, smaller than Bob but well built and sturdy. His hair was a cluster of dark curls, his cheeks as smooth and delicately carved as those of a girl. White teeth flashed in a smile that seemed ever a part of him, and his grey eyes glinted with a reckless, devil-may-care light. Bob had known him long and loved him as a brother.

They ate their suppers, cleaned up, rolled the inevitable cigarettes.

"Strange that Tomlinson isn't here yet," mused Bob. "Reckon I'll ride south a bit and try to pick up his camp fire. He cain't be far away."

Dick spoke quickly. "You'll be wastin' time, Bob. Let's have a game of stud. I got twenty dollars that's cravin' to multiply itself."

Bob ruffled the boy's hair good-naturedly. "If I sit in a game with you that twenty dollars would become a victim of division instead of multiplication. No, son, I'll ride. It won't do any harm, and I can spot Tomlinson's fire farther than you could see his drive in the dusk."

Leisurely saddling, he mounted and rode along the dim trail which threaded among the junipers and pines. Presently he reached the pass which led to the valley, and reined in to scan the floor below him. Instantly his eyes found the twinkle of a fire against the hills to the west, although Dick had reported no sign of Tomlinson and his cattle.

Bob urged his horse down the sloping trail to a point where his view of the camp site was unrestricted. Within the circle of light he could discern the outlines of three wagons; and, as if to clinch the matter, there came to him the soft lowing of cattle.

Bob turned and headed up the trail. For some reason Dick had missed the drive. In all likelihood the young man had not even scouted the valley, Bob concluded. "Dog-goned little slacker," he mused.

Pushing back through the pass, he descended into a dark hollow through which trickled a tiny stream. His horse stopped and lowered his head to drink, and Bob, slacking the reins, set to fashioning a cigarette. On the verge of striking a match he paused and stiffened. To his alert ears came the solid rhythmic thud of hoofs— many of them. And then, across the top of a ridge ahead of him, swept a band of horsemen, riding swiftly and in close formation. They showed against the sky for ten brief seconds, then were swallowed in the blackness of the hills to his left.

Bob thoughtfully returned the match to his pocket, tightened the reins, and sent his horse up the slight incline, then down the far grade at a fast lope. The four about the camp fire stared curiously as he pulled up.

"Get yore horses," he ordered briefly. "Tomlinson is camped in the valley two miles south, and I saw a dozen or more riders circlin' around to the west. They were in the hills and ridin' hard."

"What's the rush?" complained Dick.

"I don't know of any considerable bunch of riders that go tearin' through the hills at night except Kurt Dodd's rustlers. I figure they aim to jump Tomlinson, and unless we hurry we won't be a bit of good to him."

Ace, Deuce, and the Mexican ran toward the corral. For a moment Dick eyed his friend, then he smiled and shrugged.

"How many times I got to tell you Kurt ain't mixed up with that rustlin' outfit? I know him, and he's a square-shooter. Just because somebody is operatin' in the hills back of his spread—" He broke off and got to his feet. "Well, the game's busted up; might as well mosey along."

By this time the raiders had traversed the northern hills and had cut to the southeast. They rode swiftly, for the trail was well marked and comparatively easy of negotiation. Presently their leader slowed the pace of his horse and swung to the left, beginning the ascent of a steep trail which bore steadily toward a cleft in the hills above them. The darkness was thick, but the moon had risen and the pass stood out boldly against the sky.

They threaded the cleft and started down the trail which led to the valley below. On the grassy flats vigilant cowboys circled sleeping steers. Their faces tightened avidly. A little trail ga'nted, Dodd had said, but they would fatten easily!

At the foot of the incline Kurt spoke shortly. "Look to yore guns."

The moon topped the eastern range and the whole valley was flooded with its mellow light. They could see the bedded-down cattle now, occasionally they glimpsed the vague form of a rider. Borne on the gentle breeze came snatches of a range song, the words muffled by distance, the tune plaintive. Off to one side of them glowed the camp fire, a half-dozen blanketed figures surrounding it. Dodd nodded his satisfaction.

"One of them is the cook," he told Shab in a low voice. "Likely the girl sleeps in the wagon. That means only two of them are night-hawkin' at a time. It'll be easy." He turned to the men. "You boys know what to do. Start spreadin' as soon as you hit the flat. Shoot and yell from the first jump. If anybody gits in yore way, drop him. All set? Let's ride!"

Into the open they spurred, no longer careful of the sounds they made. Kurt Dodd raised his arm in a signal. Hoofs churned the earth, yells and sixgun blasts shattered the peaceful quiet; then they were sweeping in a gradually spreading line toward the herd on the valley flats.

The figures about the fire came to their feet reaching instinctively for weapons. Dodd, a watchful eye on them, dropped back from his position, and, halting his horse, drew the carbine from its boot beneath his leg. Tomlinson was running toward the freighter, calling to the girl inside. An arm holding a rifle appeared from beneath the wagon cover, followed by the head of his daughter. Kurt caught the glint of the firelight on her yellow hair.

The carbine in his hands leaped upward, followed the figure of the running man, stiffened, then spat viciously. Tomlinson went down as though his legs had been knocked from beneath him. Kurt flung another shot into the embers of the fire, then raced after his men.

The frightened cattle had come to their feet. The clash of horns and thud of bodies mingled with their bawls. Around one flank spurred a night guard, his sixgun spitting. Kurt, sighting him instantly, again raised his carbine and fired. The horse plunged into the dirt, throwing the cowboy hard. He was lying where he had fallen when Dodd rode past the place.

The panic of the foremost steers was transmitted to those farther in; they, too, turned and fought to win clear. Then the whole herd was in headlong flight, running blindly, terror-stricken. The guard on the far side was hard put to get out of their path. He drove his spurs deep and angled for the head of the valley. Once free of the threat of death beneath frantic hoofs he swung in an arc across the valley, circling for the camp fire. Near the center of the flat he jerked up his gun and fired, cursing his short-sightedness in not arming himself with a rifle.

Five men were sweeping across the valley flat from the north, and he naturally mistook them for another body of raiders. Then he caught the flash of their rifles and saw to his surprise that they were shooting at the thin line of rustlers.

In the moonlight everything was quite clear. He saw the raiders swing their horses to meet this menace, abandoning the flying cattle to converge in a little group. One of them, evidently their leader, spurred out to the front and leveled his carbine. The five rode straight on without slacking their pace, erect in their saddles, rifles flaming. One of the horses in the raiding party went down, and the rider, springing clear, seized the hand of a comrade and swung up behind him. The leader turned and made a sweeping gesture with his arm; then, while his men headed for the gullies and ravines in precipitate retreat, he fired at the approaching five until his rifle was empty, shook a futile fist, and turned to make his own escape.

"Ride that man down!" came Bob Lee's terse command. "Get him and the whole thievin' gang is broken up!"

The main body of rustlers had separated in units of two or three, all heading for the eastern hills where the gully and ravine mouths were swallowed in the gloom of the hills. The leader, however, struck obliquely across the valley in order to reach the hills at a point where he would not be impeded by the stampeding cattle.

Quite abruptly he swung his horse to the west and headed directly toward a debouching ravine. It meant lessening the distance between himself and his pursuers, but it permitted him to use the full speed of his horse clear to the mouth of the ravine.

Dick's voice sounded above the noise of their horses' hoofs. "If I can climb that cliff I can head him!" Without waiting for Bob's permission, he swung to the right and sent his horse toward the steep slant of a bluff which rose abruptly from the valley floor.

At the foot of the cliff Dick swerved his mount and

started the ascent at an angle. Lunge after lunge the horse made, his momentum carrying him far up the side of the cliff before he faltered. At precisely the right moment Dick pivoted him and sent him up on the opposite tack. The animal reached the very edge of the solid ground above, pawed frantically with his front feet.

Markley slipped from the saddle, sprang for the top, reached it; then literally dragged the horse after him. In an instant he had sprung to the saddle, waved a hand at them, and disappeared.

The rustler leader had reached the mouth of the ravine. Bob swung up his rifle and fired three swift shots which apparently missed their target. The next moment man and horse were swallowed by the gloom.

"No more shootin'," ordered Bob. "Dick's up ahead somewhere."

The footing in the ravine was treacherous and with the moonlight walled out it was inconceivably dark. They were forced to slow their pace to a walk. From some point ahead of them came a sudden shot—the boom of a sixgun.

"Got him!" exclaimed Deuce.

"Maybe," said Joe, the Mexican. "Thees other man, she have gon too."

"Hit it up," ordered Bob. The Mexican was right; this outlaw leader, as desperate as he was fearless, was also armed, and he would shoot to kill.

Five minutes later they rounded a bend in the ravine and pulled up sharply. Ahead of them gleamed a pinpoint of light, the glow of a cigarette.

Dick's voice came to them out of the darkness. "It's me."

They rode forward a dozen paces and dismounted. Bob struck a match. Dick was seated on a rock beside the body of a horse.

"Where's the rider?" asked Ace. "And where's yore cayuse?"

"Both gone," answered Dick calmly. "I saw him foggin' along the ravine and shot his horse. Rider went down hard and I thought he was stunned. It's so danged dark that I couldn't find him, and he jumped me from behind. Took my horse and vamosed."

"Who was he?" asked Deuce.

"I don't know. Too dark to see."

Bob slapped him on the back. "Good old Dick! You took a chance, boy; he might have got you. . . . Well, no use followin'. Reckon we'd better join Tomlinson and see what damage was done. You can ride behind me, Dick."

Ace was on his haunches examining the dead horse. He looked up to find Deuce and the Mexican standing beside him. Bob and Dick were already on their way out of the ravine.

"What did you find?" asked Deuce in a low voice.

"Shot plumb between the eyes."

"Huh! Must 'a' been a accident, to put a slug there in the dark."

"It was a accident all right." Ace struck another match and, grasping the right foreleg of the horse, moved it gently. "The accident came when the horse fell and broke his leg. He was shot afterwards."

The three exchanged glances. "And Dick said Tomlinson wasn't in the valley," mused Deuce. "I'd shore like to take this critter's upper works apart and examine that slug. Dick shoots a forty-one, and my in-too-ition tells me this horse was plugged with a forty-five."

The Mexican swore softly. *"Madre de Dios!* And Bob ees call heem 'Good ol' Deek!'"

Chapter II

MURDER AT THE RED FRONT

THE three discussed the matter as they rode slowly after Bob and Dick.

"This shore jars me," said Deuce. "What are we goin' to tell Bob?"

"Nothin'," answered Ace. "He wouldn't believe us. For him the sun rises and sets in Dick Markley."

"But, dang it! he oughta know." Deuce glanced toward the Mexican.

Joe shrugged. "Bob mus' fin' out for heemself. We have only w'at you call sus-pee-cion. We theenk 'orse ees fall and break hees leg; we theenk thees rus'ler eshoot heem; we theenk that Deek ees give heem hees own *caballo*. We *theenk* that; but we do not know. *Señor* Bob weel not believe."

"He'll believe if I dig a forty-one slug outa that horse's head!"

"He weel say maybe thees outlaw ees eshoot forty-one also."

"Joe's right," agreed Ace. "The only thing we can do is sit tight and watch. Dang Dick Markley anyhow!"

They found the two awaiting them at the mouth of the ravine, and rode swiftly and in silence across the valley toward Tomlinson's camp fire. As they drew near, a rifle barked and its slug whined over their heads. They pulled up and Bob called his identity across the intervening space.

Continuing to the wagons, they dismounted. Tomlinson was seated with his back against a tree, one leg supported by a pillow. Near him stood a girl with a rifle, and at sight of her all five stopped and stared.

Never had Bob seen a girl just like her. Western, by her rig and the way she handled the weapon, yet different from any sun-browned daughter of the range he had ever known. Perhaps it was the pure gold of her hair beneath the white Stetson, or the dark brows and lashes which contrasted so strikingly with her fair skin. Perhaps it was the slender delicacy of her lissom form or the erect, almost jaunty, way she carried her head. Pretty was too frail a word with which to describe her; beautiful, not sufficiently all-covering.

Dick's low exclamation aroused Bob. Markley had swept his hat from his head and was staring at her with bold, admiring eyes. Bob removed his own Stetson and stepped forward.

"Good evenin', Miss. Evenin', Mr. Tomlinson. You badly hurt?"

"Broken leg," replied the Texan. "June, this is Bob Lee."

The girl smiled. "I'm glad to know you, Mr. Lee. Father tells me you are from Texas, too."

"Yes, ma'am. Meet Charley Talbot, Harry Lowery, José Villegas, and Dick Markley, ma'am. The first three are from Texas also. Dick isn't, but he tries hard to make up for it."

"Proud to meetcha, ma'am," gulped Ace.

"Same here," mumbled Deuce.

José bowed, teeth gleaming. "Ees ver' gr-r-reat pleasure."

Dick stepped forward and took her hand. His eyes were dancing. "I'm a sinful man," he told her gravely, "but that's because I never before knew just what an angel looked like. I'm reformin' from this moment."

Bob turned to her father. "We chased the leader of the crowd into the hills. He got away from us. Did yore men have any better luck?"

"I reckon not. They shore caught us flat-footed. We had to catch up horses, and by that time it was all over."

The Tomlinson crew rode up and dismounted. The guard whose horse had been shot was riding behind a companion. The fall had rendered him unconscious, but except for a superficial head wound he was uninjured.

"I'll ride to Lariat for a doctor," June said. "Dad needs one badly."

"If yore father will lend me a horse, I'll ride with you," offered Dick.

"I wish you would," Tomlinson said. "You know the country. Take yore pick of the *remuda*."

Dick and the girl moved away from the fire, and presently Bob heard the drum of hoofs and caught a brief glimpse of the pair as they rode northward.

Tomlinson stoically retained his position against the tree. He was a big, ruddy-faced, heavy-mustached man —a pioneer, inured to hardship. Despite the pain, he went about introducing the four to his crew and listened to his foreman's report. Unfamiliar with the terrain, they had not established contact with a single rustler. The cattle were scattered in a dozen gullies and ravines.

They put up their horses and dropped beside the fire. Bob went about making Tomlinson comfortable. He found an opiate in the medicine chest, and administered enough to make the Texan drowsy. When Tomlinson had closed his eyes, Bob rejoined his companions. They were discussing Dick and the girl.

"He always was lucky," sighed Ace.

"Don't blame it on luck," said Deuce peevishly. "If you had half his gall you'd 'a' offered to ride to town with her."

"You weren't overflowin' with words yoreself. All you done was mumble 'Same here' and stand starin' like a sick calf."

José Villegas sighed dolorously. "Me, I'm theenk I'm w'at you call in the loff."

Deuce turned to him in amazement. "Why, you black-eyed son of sin! You go twangin' that gui-tar under *her* window and I'll wrap it around yore neck!"

Bob grinned as he rolled himself in his blanket. "Reckon you're all sort of premature. Here you are fallin' in love with a lady and not one of you can tell me the color of her eyes."

"They are blue," stated Deuce.

"You're color blind," sniffed Ace. "They're brown."

"Me, I'm theenk they are black lak the night."

Bob spoke with his back turned. "Wait until mornin' and see." But he knew all the while that they were violet; deep, fathomless, soul-stirring. And through the night they haunted him until at last he kicked free of the blanket and sat by the dying embers smoking until dawn.

June and Dick arrived with Doc Witherspoon just as the crew, supplemented by Bob and his friends, were about to start after the cattle.

"Me, I'm good from feex the leg which is bus'," suggested Joe. "I'm stay weeth the *señorita* and help the *medico*."

"You'll start after them cows with the rest of the fellas," Dick told him. "I'll do all the helpin' that's necessary. Who went after that doctor, anyhow? Besides, I haven't had my breakfast. Get goin'."

"Danged upstart!" muttered Deuce as they started for their horses. "How's he get that way—givin' us orders!"

"He mus' have hees leetle moment," said Joe. "Wait till I'm get my guitar; I'm show heem how we mak the loff in old *Mejico*."

"You try it and I'll show you how we make the hash in New Mexico!"

By noon the cattle were once more bunched in the valley. The doctor had departed, and Tomlinson was resting comfortably. That afternoon they drove north over the pass, and two days later found the cattle safely on what had been the Wagonwheel, Bob's old spread. Here had been gathered the stock sold to Tomlinson by Lee and John Rutherford. The animals were tallied and the work of rebranding began. Tomlinson, unable to direct the work himself, hired Bob to assist his foreman, retaining at the same time Bob's old crew. John Rutherford was the Cleanup Party's candidate for sheriff, and left for a swing around the county immediately after an accounting had been rendered.

The end of the week saw order established, with every animal on the spread bearing the Tumbling T of the new owner. June Tomlinson had worked with the boys, all of whom thought themselves in love with her. Ace and Deuce were abashed and more or less tongue-tied in her presence. Joe sighed often and wished repeatedly for his guitar. Dick was ever at her side, anticipating every wish, grinning that devil-may-care grin, joking with her, teasing her.

Bob gave no outward indication of his feelings. Dick had monopolized her company, and Dick was his friend. If, on occasion, he experienced a little pang of jealousy, he smothered it instantly under a blanket of cold fact.

"Keep yore feet on the ground, cowboy," he would tell himself. "She's young: nineteen or twenty; Dick is twenty-three. Just right. You're almost thirty. And the kid has the inside of the track. You're no poacher. Keep yore feet on the ground and yore head out of the clouds."

It was Monday afternoon—the day before election —when they finally bade the Tomlinsons good-by and rode into Lariat. The town was humming, with every man who could be spared from the range on hand for the election. Saloons and gambling joints were running at top speed. Dismounting and tying at the hitching rack before the Paris Hotel and Saloon, the four stepped to the plank sidewalk, an oddly assorted group.

A traveling salesman seated on the hotel veranda eyed them curiously and turned to his companion for information. Pop Purvis, retired cattleman, spat and enlightened him.

"Them there are the former owner and crew of the old Wagonwheel. Right now they're on the loose, Bob Lee havin' sold out to a Texan named Tomlinson. Bob drove some cows up from Texas three, four years ago. The Mexican, Joe Villegas, came with him. When he'd got a start, he sent for the other two. The high altitude fella is named Talbot; the short one is Harry Lowery. They been travelin' together so long folks got to callin' 'em Ace and Deuce. Bob Lee, I reckon, is the jack."

"Sounds like a game of seven-up."

"Seven-up is right. The Mex ain't no slouch; he stacks up a ten-spot anyhow, and that counts right smart towards game. Seven-up she is, with high, low, jack, and game in one hand. You cain't beat that!"

"And the other lad?"

"Dick Markley? Well, I'd call him a sort of joker. Wild young buck, always gettin' in trouble and makin' Bob git him out. Never seen a fella cotton to another like Bob has to Dick. Jest like a big brother, only closer."

The five, in the meanwhile, had passed into the Paris saloon. While the other three elbowed their way to the bar, Bob and Dick paused by a roulette wheel to watch the play. Suddenly Dick swore and turned away. Bob followed him, wondering, and when he joined him at the bar spoke quietly.

"What's worryin' you, old son?"

Dick shrugged impatiently. "I don't know. I reckon it was that pile of gold on the roulette table. I was

thinkin' what I could do with it. Here I am reachin'
the point where I ought to think of marryin' and havin'
a little spread of my own, and what have I got?
Ten dollars, a horse, and a saddle! Not even a job.
And plenty of cheap-skate gamblers and bloated bank-
ers and hard-shell cattle barons with more than they
can ever use."

"You're young," began Bob, but Dick interrupted
him harshly.

"Young hell! I'm twenty-three. If I'm to get anywhere it's time I was makin' a start." He downed his
drink and turned away. "See you later. Got business
with a fella."

Bob frowned thoughtfully. Dick was in love with
June Tomlinson and had begun to realize that he
possessed very little to offer the girl of his choice.
Perhaps the realization was a good thing for him. If
the feeling he entertained for June was genuine, he
would buckle down and make something of himself.

Somebody tugged at his sleeve and Bob turned his
head to see Ace.

"Let's get out of here," suggested the tall cowboy.
"It's too danged crowded. How about the Red Front?"

Bob backed through the mob into the open and
glanced about the room. At a table sat two men, talking.
One was Dick, the other was Duke Haslam, owner of
the Paris. Bidding Ace wait, Bob approached the pair.

"Hello, Duke," he said. "Don't aim to horn in; just
wanted to tell Dick that he'll find us at the Red
Front."

Dick nodded. "I'll be over in a few minutes."

Haslam removed a cigar from his mouth and asked a

question. "You'll be in town for the election tomorrow, Bob?"

"I reckon so." Bob's answer was a bit short. He did not like Duke Haslam; never had and never would, although he was fair enough to admit that his dislike was based entirely on prejudice. Duke was heavy-set, well-dressed, and prosperous-appearing. His sleek black hair was plastered against his forehead in the prevailing mode, and his dark mustache was carefully waxed and curled. The lips were full, the eyes a bit too close together. To Bob he seemed oily; too much like a snake.

Haslam went on. "I've been talking to Dick about the election. We need the support of every good man. This so-called Cleanup Party has taken in a lot of gullible folk. John Rutherford is all right, but he is getting along in years and he hasn't the experience of Peter Grubb. Grubb is a good sheriff, honest and fearless in the performance of his—"

"Pete Grubb," interrupted Bob, "is crooked and would run from his own shadow. If you don't believe it, tell him what I said and see what he does."

Haslam's face slowly reddened. "You have no call to speak that way of him. Grubb is efficient—"

Again Bob cut him short. "Grubb is a weak-kneed sister without enough backbone to stand up to a horny toad. I'm talkin' plain, Duke. You're a politician, and just about run Lariat. Well, go ahead and run her as long as you can get away with it. But when you try to tell me Pete Grubb is efficient and honest and fearless, I'm tellin' you that you're talkin' through yore Stetson."

"Then I take it that you're supporting Rutherford?"

"You take it correctly. Ever since Grubb has been in office, that outlaw, Kurt Dodd, has been runnin' wild."

"You can't prove that Dodd runs that outfit."

"If I could, he wouldn't be runnin' it long! Cattlemen have lost stock, banks and stages have been robbed. Grubb has had two years in which to round up the bunch, but what has he done? Nothin'—plus! He gets on a horse, makes war talk to a posse, and goes chasin' around in the hills. Supper time finds him back in town lookin' sad and tellin' what he'll do the next time. John Rutherford has been rustled blind. So have I. That's the main reason for our sellin' out. By watchin' night and day I could save my stock, but I refuse to run myself into bankruptcy by hirin' a double crew. Yes, sir; you can bet yore boots I'm supportin' Rutherford."

Haslam rose and leaned across the table so that only inches separated their faces. His voice was pitched quite low, but there was no mistaking his earnestness. "I'll do some plain talking myself. Lee, this is a bad climate for some folks. You've sold out to Tomlinson, so there is nothing to hold you in Lariat. All kind of distance extends to the north, east, south, and west; there are undoubtedly wonderful opportunities for a young man with newly acquired capital. My advice to you is to get out of Lariat, and to get out while the getting is good."

Lee smiled tightly. "And if I fail to take that advice?"

Haslam's eyes were narrowed and glinting. "Then I'm afraid you'll never vote in tomorrow's election."

"Duke, I always was a curious cuss! You plumb intrigue me. Yes, sir. Now I just got to stay to see how true a prophet you are. And that regardless of the golden opportunities awaitin' me north, south, east, and west."

For another moment their gazes locked—held. There was a little smile on Bob's lips, although his eyes were cold. Haslam stood rigidly, jaws tightly clamped. Suddenly he relaxed and shrugged.

"You're a fool," he said shortly, and resumed his seat.

Bob joined his friends, who had watched the exchange from a place near the door.

"What's eatin' his elegance?" inquired Deuce as they pushed through the swinging doors.

"He's riled because I disputed his claims in favor of honest, efficient, fearless Pete Grubb."

Deuce snorted. " 'Mouldy' Grubb honest? Why that hairpin is so crooked he leaves a track like a clock spring."

They mounted their horses and rode down the street toward the Red Front. Presently they were forced to pull to one side to permit the passage of a half-dozen horsemen. Leading them was a big, black-bearded giant of a man.

"Kurt Dodd," said Deuce. "Come to help elect his friend, Mouldy Grubb."

"The danged cowthief!" growled Ace.

The others mentally agreed with him. Ostensibly Dodd was a rancher, his spread extending far back into the foothills. There were hidden parks within the limits of his domain where cattle could be held until worked-over brands had healed, or where loot from bank and stage could be concealed until danger of detection had passed. Many and devious trails crossed and criss-crossed his holdings—trails which would serve admirably to confuse pursuing posses.

Kurt was in the Red Front when Bob and his friends entered. He was standing before the long bar, drinking and talking with the weak-kneed Pete Grubb. Mouldy was nodding approval of something Dodd was saying. He was as lacking in personality as a sack of bran, weak of chin, lackluster of eye, insignificant in both size and bearing.

"And that," muttered Ace, "is what Duke Haslam wants us to vote for!"

"There's the man gets my vote," said Deuce.

He nodded toward the far end of the bar. John Rutherford was talking with two cattlemen, Frank Enright of the Big 4 and Dutch Trumbauer, who owned the Candlestick. Rutherford was in his late sixties, tall and broad and florid, with close-cropped gray mustache and grizzled hair. A pair of dark, hawk-like eyes peered from beneath shaggy brows. A blind man could have sensed his superiority to Pete Grubb.

The Cleanup Party's candidate turned at their approach.

"Howdy, Bob; howdy, boys. Glad to see you-all. Belly up here. I ain't much on electioneerin' but I am buyin' the drinks."

"We're for you drinks or no drinks," Bob told him. "How's the outlook?"

Frank Enright answered. "Mighty fine, Bob. If

everybody votes like they promised, John is as good as elected."

"Theese Duke Haslam," observed Joe, "ees one foxy *hombre*. May be she have w'at you call the treek up my sleeve, no?"

"It no difference makes vat trick he hass his sleeve up," said Dutch Trumbauer. "Dis time it iss der people vat speak, ain't it, Frank?"

"You told the truth that time, Dutch. The voice of the people is callin' for a change, and it's callin' mighty loud."

Bob raised his glass. "Well, here's to success."

Rutherford followed suit. "Thanks, Bob. I shore appreciate—"

Behind them came the roar of a sixgun and the tinkle of glass. Rutherford's big frame jerked spasmodically, his jaw went slack; then the sturdy knees gave beneath him and he slid slowly downward along the face of the bar.

Chapter III

OUT OF THE NIGHT

Bob whipped his gun from its holster and wheeled. On the far side of the room smoke eddied about a broken window. He fired a shot through the opening, then desisted as Deuce sprang across the intervening space and hurtled through the lower sash, taking the rest of the glass with him.

Ace followed. Joe was running toward the door which opened on an alley. Bob pushed through the petrified crowd to the front door and thence to the street. Glancing quickly about, he strode to the dark passageway beside the saloon. From somewhere in the rear of the place came the sound of two heavy shots, and he broke into a run. A vague figure appeared at the far corner of the building.

"That you, Bob? Bring the horses—quick!" It was Deuce.

Racing to the rack, Bob flipped the reins free and led the horses into the alley. Deuce met him.

"Joe and Ace are after him. Gimme my cayuse."

They leaped into their saddles and, each leading a horse, spurred around the rear corner. The forms of Ace and Joe loomed up in the darkness. Grasping the reins which were flung to them, they leaped astride their mounts.

"He's still in the alley," Ace shouted. "Keep crowdin' him!"

They sped along the dark passageway and past the straggling buildings at the edge of town. At Bob's command they halted. From some point ahead came the steady drum of hoofs. They spurred in pursuit. Presently they again pulled up. The roll of hoofbeats flung back at them in swifter cadence. The murderer knew that his pursuers were crowding him and was becoming panicky.

Slowly Bob and the Mexican forged ahead. Straight on they rode at the very top of their mounts' speed; and then Bob caught sight of a dim figure some two hundred yards ahead. It was vague and shapeless, but it moved, and he knew it to be a man and a horse, the former leaning far over the animal's neck. Joe caught sight of him at the same time.

The killer swerved his mount in an effort to throw them off. Immediately Joe kneed his horse at an angle that would intercept him. The fellow turned in the opposite direction only to have Bob cut down the distance between them. Desperately he started throwing lead, turning in his saddle and shooting at random in the hope of scaring them off.

Foot by foot they cut down the space between them and their quarry, maintaining such positions that should the fellow bolt off at an angle one or the other would be able to head him. They were a hundred feet behind him now and drawing closer at every bound. Seventy-five feet—fifty. Joe was whirling his riata, and there wasn't a better roper north of the Rio Grande.

Forty feet, and then thirty. The rope flicked out, its noose settling around the extended neck of the horse and the leaning form of the man. They swung off to the left, stopped. Joe held his rope taut while Bob rode up on the far side. Their man was helpless, bound securely to his horse.

Bob reached over, jerked the gun from the fellow's unresisting fingers, felt him over swiftly for other weapons. Working silently but efficiently he bound the fellow's hands to the saddle horn and was tying his feet beneath the belly of the horse when Ace and Deuce rode up.

"Why didn't you plug the skunk?" demanded Deuce hotly.

"We're not sure that John is dead. Reckon we'll take him back to Lariat."

They found the town in a turmoil which turned almost to frenzy as they rode down the street with their prisoner. Men surged about their horses, snatching at the fellow, cursing him. Nobody seemed to know him.

John Rutherford was dead; shot through the heart.

Bob's face tightened at the news, but he spoke sharply to his companions and the four completely surrounded the cowering prisoner. As they passed the hotel, Bob saw Duke Haslam standing on the veranda. The gasoline flare at the entrance lighted his smug countenance as he puffed languidly at his cigar, a hint of sardonic amusement in his eyes. A sudden hot rage sprang up within Bob.

Before the Red Front the party halted, and Lee held up his arm for silence. Glancing over the crowd, he

singled out Sheriff Pete Grubb, who was edging unobtrusively toward the saloon entrance.

"Sheriff, I've brought you the man who murdered
John Rutherford. I'm handin' him over to the law."

Grubb halted, turned, came hesitatingly through the
crowd. "You ain't been deputized," he protested
weakly.

Bob did not trouble to answer. Reaching down, he
cut the thong which bound the fellow's ankles, then
severed the one which fastened his hands to the saddle.
Gripping the killer under the arms, he lifted him
from the saddle and dropped him at Grubb's feet. The
fellow stumbled and fell to his knees.

Grubb never put a hand on him. Frank Enright
grasped the sheriff by coat collar and breeches slack
and tossed him to one side. Bending over, he yanked
the murderer to his feet.

"A heap of folks were John's friends," he said simply. "I'm one of them. I reckon this polecat belongs
to us."

The Mexican's teeth showed in a sudden smile.
Swiftly untying his lariat he passed it to the cowman.
"Thees ees ver' fine riata; good and strong. I'm frien'
of John Ruddafo'd too."

Enright nodded and took the proffered rope. Dutch
Trumbauer gripped the killer by an arm. Whimpering
and pleading, the man was hustled along the street,
Ace, Deuce, and the Mexican riding with the crowd.
Bob watched them surge into the livery barn with its
overhead rafters, then rode to the hitching rack, dismounted, and entered the Red Front. Besides the pro-

prietor there was but one other man in the room. It was Dick Markley.

Dick spoke gravely. "Well, pore old John won't run for sheriff after all."

"No. John didn't have a chance against a bullet from behind."

"Shore is tough. But it just goes to show that you cain't buck the powers that be."

Bob ordered a bottle of beer and drank it thoughtfully. Through open doors and windows he could hear the shouts of the frenzied mob in the livery barn. The excited cries were followed by a volley of revolver shots. Mentally Bob pictured the dangling, swaying body of the killer, leaden slugs ripping into a torso already past feeling.

Dick suddenly turned and gripped Bob by an arm. "Partner, Duke has it in for you. Listen to me. Do what he advised: get out of Lariat and stay out!"

"Turn tail to Duke Haslam? Not so's you'd notice it! I'm beginnin' to have ideas about that jasper. I—"

He was interrupted by a loud shout from the lynchers. Bob strode to the doorway, Dick at his heels. A noisy procession came down the street, some of its members carrying lanterns, other waving torches. They halted before the Red Front and surged in a shouting, cheering mob about the two men who stood just inside the entrance. Frank Enright pushed through the crowd and stood before Bob. Instantly the noise subsided.

"Bob Lee," he said, his voice ringing with earnestness, "when that measly little killer was paid to rub out pore old John, the ones who hired him figgered that they were killin' the Cleanup Party at the same time. But back there under the gallows the citizens of this county decided that the party ain't ready to die, but is goin' to live until the real murderer is brought to justice. Bob Lee, we're nominatin' you our candidate for sheriff, and by the mem'ry of John Rutherford, you're goin' to win!"

With the last ringing words, pandemonium broke loose. Men shouted and clapped each other on the back; those near enough seized Bob's hand and wrung it. Sixguns roared skyward.

"Speech!" yelled somebody, a demand that was swiftly taken up by others. Before Bob realized what they were about, he found himself raised in the air and planted upon a shaky box which had materialized from somewhere. The whole thing was so entirely unexpected that for the moment he was disconcerted.

What they suggested was impossible, he told himself. He had neither the desire for such a thankless job nor the incentive of greed which might prompt him to accept the position for what he could get out of it. It was with the intention of refusing the nomination that he raised his hand for silence.

And then, from somewhere up the street a rifle flamed, its spiteful crack sounding plainly above the noise made by the crowd. Bob's hat slipped sidewise on his head, the flimsy box collapsed beneath him, and he was thrown into the dust near the hitching rack.

A yell of mingled consternation and rage went up from the crowd. Ace, Deuce, and Joe forced their mounts through the milling mob toward their friend, only to see him leap to his feet unhurt. Instantly they wheeled their horses toward the point from which the shot had come, sweeping each dark passage, scouring street and alley. Others who were mounted followed.

Dick had seized Bob by an arm and was shaking him. "Bob, for God's sake do what I told you! Make tracks now! Man, cain't you see what's goin' to happen if you stay? Get on that horse and ride!"

Bob's Stetson had fallen in the dirt; now he picked it up and pointed to the holes which punctured the crown. "If I hadn't made up my mind to stay, this would decide me. Steady me when I climb up on the hitching rack."

Dick swore wildly. "No! Good Lord, Bob, are you crazy?"

"The danger is over. Help me up."

Dick stared at him a moment longer, then, with a bitter curse, turned and walked swiftly away. Frank Enright and Dutch Trumbauer had pushed to Lee's side, and nodded soberly at his request. Bob sprang to the long rail, and, as they steadied him, again raised his hand for silence. The crowd stilled.

The words he had chosen to refuse the nomination stuck in his throat. In his mind's eye he saw again that startled, shocked expression on Rutherford's face as the fatal bullet struck him; he recalled the suave, placid countenance of Duke Haslam, smoking on the hotel porch.

When finally he did speak, it was in a low, tense voice which carried to every one in the assemblage. "I accept the nomination! Put me in office and I'll try to do what I know John Rutherford would have done had he lived to be elected."

More yells and hand-shaking and pistol shots; then the mob was swarming into the Red Front, the search for the would-be assassin abandoned. Bob did not remain long. In accordance with time-honored custom, he treated the crowd and accepted a cigar or two in return; then he slipped unobtrusively through the doorway. Dick was standing on the walk outside, and Bob threw an arm about his shoulders and drew him into the shadow of the saloon.

"Old son, I've accepted the nomination, and with the people in their present mood I've a good chance of bein' elected. If I am, I want you for a deputy. How about it?"

Dick's handsome features were drawn; for a long minute he stared out across the deserted street. "I don't know, Bob." He turned to his friend and spoke vehemently. "I wish you'd taken Duke's advice and got out of town. Now you're committed; you cain't back out. Bob, you're a marked man. And Duke said you'd never vote tomorrow."

Bob chuckled. "Well, he was a good prophet. I'm not crooked enough to vote for myself, and it's a cinch I won't vote for Mouldy Grubb."

"You don't seem to get it," said Dick impatiently. "Don't you realize how much depends on this election? They'll kill you!"

Bob dismissed the subject with a shrug. "How about that deputy job?"

"I don't know; I'll have to think it over."

"Keno. Well, reckon I'll turn in. So long, son."

Dick muttered a "so long" and turned away. He had not appeared enthused over the prospect of becoming a deputy, but Bob supposed that Markley was still upset over his close call. The knowledge that Dick was really concerned warmed Bob. Good boy, Dick Markley! Wild and impulsive, but true blue.

The distance to the Paris Hotel was short, but Bob was very much on the alert, ready to dodge and go into action should a bullet come crashing out of the darkness. Nothing happened. He put his horse in the hotel stable, entered the rear door, and made his way through the dark dining-room to the lobby. The clerk behind the counter gave him the half pitying look one might bestow on a man whose death warrant had already been signed; Duke Haslam, the only other person in sight, eyed him imperturbably, still sucking on his cigar.

"I'm stayin' in town tonight," Bob told the clerk. "Got a room for me?"

"Yes, sir. There is a nice one in front—"

Haslam interrupted him. "That front room is engaged. I forgot to tell you. Give Mr. Lee number six."

The clerk stared for a moment, then hurriedly turned and took a key from the board. Bob accepted it and tossed a dollar on the counter. "Never mind showin' me up; I can find the way."

"To the right of the stairs," Haslam told him. "You can't miss it. . . . Too bad about Rutherford, isn't it?"

"It is. Duke, somebody's goin' to pay for that murder."

Haslam's eyebrows went up. "I understood that somebody has already paid."

"They hanged the fellow who pulled the trigger; the real murderer is still at large. I am to find him whether or not I'm elected."

"You don't say! Tread warily, my lad, or you might be stopping lead yourself. Better take my advice about those wide open spaces to the north, east, south, and west." Haslam's smile was sardonic.

Bob went upstairs, unlocked the door of number six, and entered the room. Lighting the kerosene lamp, he looked about him. The furniture consisted of a bed, a chair, and a wash-stand which held, besides the lamp, a huge bowl and pitcher. The room was on the south side of the building, and was shaded by a live-oak tree, the limbs of which extended almost to the window ledge.

He stood gazing absently through the window, thinking. Haslam had lied about the other room being engaged; the surprise of the clerk was evidence of that. Removing his hat Bob examined it thoughtfully. The hole in one side of the crown was slightly higher than that on the other, showing that the bullet had ranged downward.

Going out into the hall, Bob made his way to the front of the building. The door to the corner room was locked, but the one adjoining it opened to his touch. He struck a match and by its light located the door connecting the two rooms. It was bolted on his side. Bob opened it and stepped into the corner room. At once he noticed that both windows were tightly closed. Crossing to the one in the side wall, he peered through it. Across the false front of the one-story building beside the hotel he could see the illuminated entrance to the Red Front. A man mounted on a box immediately outside the place would make an excellent target!

Bob struck a match, shielding it in his cupped palms. A quick glance about the sparsely furnished room disclosed no weapon. He snuffed out the flame, moved over to the bed, and, kneeling, thrust his hand between mattress and spring. His groping fingers came into contact with the steel barrel of a rifle.

Nodding in grim satisfaction, Bob got to his feet and moved silently from the room. The shot which had so narrowly missed him was fired from that side window, and in his mind there was no doubt as to the identity of the would-be assassin. Duke Haslam had seen his opportunity and had taken it.

Bob returned to his room, bolted the door, and swiftly undressed. His eyes occasionally strayed to the open window, but the tree outside blocked his view. Presently he extinguished the light and moved over to the bed. . . .

In the shadows at the rear of the adjoining building a man stood watching the glow which filtered through the foliage of the live-oak. When the lamplight from Bob's window at last blinked into nothingness, the fellow wiped his palms nervously on a dirty calfskin vest, hitched his belt, and stole swiftly to the tree. An empty keg was upended at the base of the trunk, and by standing upon it he could just reach the lowermost limb. Very cautiously he worked his way up among the branches, pausing to listen after each stealthy movement. No sound came from the opaque oblong which marked the window of Bob's room.

He reached the proper level at last, wedged his foot

in a crotch, and leaned back against the trunk of the tree. Silence; deep, oppressive. The man peered toward that black rectangle, trying to pierce the inner darkness of the room. He could barely discern the vague outline of the side of the bed. He drew his sixgun, leveled it, held it steady. Then he lowered it with an impatient shake of the head. Couldn't be sure; better wait for the moon.

For what seemed an interminable time he clung there in the darkness, occasionally shifting his position to ease his cramped feet. At last the sky brightened, the blackness immediately beyond the window seemed slightly to dissolve; then the last fleeting cloud was swept from the face of the moon and the man in the tree was afforded a full view of the bed within the room.

Again he raised the sixgun. He was exactly on a level with the edge of the sheet-covered mattress. Six inches higher for the first shot, he swiftly calculated, and about two feet from the head of the bed. At that range he could not miss.

He tensed, thumbed the hammer, and six rapid shots shattered the midnight stillness.

CHAPTER IV

THE TEMPTER

AT THE sound of the first crashing shot, Bob leaped from the blanket he had spread on the floor, his sixgun in hand. Crouching at the end of the room he counted the reports: one, two, three, four, five, six!

A moment's pause to be sure the would-be killer had only one gun, then he sprang to the window. The tree was a large one; no swaying limb betrayed the position of the attacker. Bob fired into the heart of the foliage and was rewarded by hearing a smothered exclamation. Then came the sound of a falling body, a thud, and the pound of fleeing footsteps. An instant later the rapid drum of hoofbeats flung back at him, then came silence.

Bob quickly reloaded his gun and, running to the door, unbarred it. Somebody was rapidly mounting the stairs. He lighted the lamp and turned to face the entrance. The door opened, and Duke Haslam burst into the room, eyes fixed on the bed. Sensing Bob's presence, he wheeled, and for the first time Lee saw him lose control of that mask-like face.

"Anxious about me?" inquired Bob.

"Why, I—I—" Haslam recovered his poise with an effort. "Yes, I was. I warned you that you might stop lead, and on top of my warning I heard those shots. I thought they'd got you."

"Sort of a strange coincidence, wasn't it?" Bob walked over to the bed, threw back the covers. "I didn't like the looks of that tree, and I remembered yore warnin'; so I sacrificed comfort for safety and slept on the floor. Unfortunately I had to use yore wash-stand pitcher for a head on this dummy, and the bowl for part of the body. They shore are busted up."

Boots again pounded the stair steps and Ace, Deuce, and Joe rushed into the room. They appeared vastly relieved to see Bob apparently unhurt. Moving over to the bed they looked at the ripped covers, at the tree outside, and then at the blanket and pillow on the floor.

Joe grinned. "Thees sheriff, she have the hard life. Weeth good bed and soft mattress, Bob ees slip on the floor."

"Good thing he did," murmured Deuce, "or he'd do the rest of his sleepin' under a blanket of daisies. Reckon I'll bed down in the hall the rest of the night."

"And I'll curl up at the foot of that tree," decided Ace. "Bob's an important person now, and one dead candidate a night is plenty."

Bob spoke to Haslam. "You can go to bed now, Duke. Don't worry so much about me; I reckon I'll last the night out."

Duke eyed him levelly for a few seconds, then turned and walked from the room. Ace and Deuce followed him, and Joe proceeded to remove his boots.

"The barn ees lock' after the *caballo* she ees go.

Me, I'm won'er w'ere I'm slip tonight, and here I'm fin' good bed! Come, *amigo;* breeng the blanket and the peelow. We catch w'at you call the good snooze, no?"

Bob Lee was elected sheriff the next day. It was an orderly election as elections go, for cowboys from the ranches of law-abiding cattlemen remained on the job in the courthouse with Kurt Dodd and his gunmen, and saw to it that voters were neither influenced nor molested. When the result was announced that night, Kurt Dodd swore savagely and kicked a hole in the ballot box, while Duke Haslam clamped his teeth on his cigar so tightly that his jaw muscles stood out in ridges.

Bob drew Dick Markley to one side. "I want to talk to you about that deputy job. Dick, it pays a hundred a month. It will put you on yore feet, and in time you— you—" He broke off, a bit dismayed to find that the words came so hard.

Markley nodded. "I know. I want to make money, Bob, so I can offer June somethin' besides my name; but I got somethin' else in view. So long, and take care of yoreself." He seemed anxious to get away.

The actual swearing in of the new sheriff took place the next day. The county judge and the prosecuting attorney, both Haslam men, had been re-elected, the Cleanup Party concentrating its efforts on the office of sheriff.

Judge Bleek was tall, thin, and dyspeptic. His indigestion had soured him on the world, and it was the general opinion that the unlucky man who faced him in his court during one of his "spells" would receive the limit regardless of whether or not he was backed by Haslam. Thaddeus Poole, the prosecuting attorney, was fifty-five, fat, and fond of oratory. When sober he was a dignified old bluffer. That he had more than a casual acquaintance with the demon rum was attested by his blue-veined cheeks and ruddy nose.

The ceremony over, Bob took possession of the sheriff's office, receiving keys, badges, handcuffs, and other appurtenances from the former sheriff. Here he swore in as deputies Ace, Deuce, and Joe, after which the four seated themselves to talk over a plan of campaign.

"There are two problems ahead of us," Bob told them. "One is to pin the deadwood on the jasper who ordered the death of Rutherford, the other is to break up the gang which has been stealin' the folks of this country blind."

"If you ask me," volunteered Deuce, "the two are linked together like twin sausages."

"Who do you figure had John murdered?"

"Duke Haslam. By murderin' John right before election he figgered the Cleanup Party wouldn't be able to find another candidate in time to run."

"You said the murder of Rutherford was connected with the stealin' and killin' that have been goin' on. If that is so, and Haslam had John killed, he must also be runnin' the outlaw band."

"I don't know about that," said Ace. "Folks sorta

figger Kurt Dodd to be what you might call the prime mover of that outfit."

The Mexican spoke positively. "Duke Haslam ees behin' eet all."

"How come?"

"Thees keeler we hang, she ees hire' by Duke. *Bueno*. Nobody know heem; she ees not leave in town and she does not work on any *rancho* we know. Yet she mus' eat and slip. So she work for Dodd, no?"

"Sounds reasonable."

"*Bueno!* Now she work for Dodd, but she keel for Haslam; so Dodd and Haslam ees work together."

Deuce swore admiringly. "That was my hunch, but I'm danged if I could put it so clear. Joe, you win the han'some crocheted spurs."

"I believe Joe is right," said Bob. "At any rate we'll find out pretty quick. If Duke isn't behind the whole thing, the one who is will lie low until he sees which way the wind blows. If Haslam is the real leader, we can look for the lightnin' to strike real sudden."

"That's plumb correct," agreed Ace. "He'll do his dangdest to make us look foolish so he can tell folks how much better Grubb would 'a' done."

"And since we don't know where the blow will be aimed, we must split our forces. Joe, after dinner you get a blanket roll and some grub and camp along the road twenty miles north of Lariat. Follow the stage in tomorrow. Circle the town and pick it up on the other side when it leaves. Trail it twenty miles south and wait for the north-bound. Keep that up until further orders.

"Deuce, you and Ace ride range. Sleep in the daytime and prowl around at night. I'll stay in town. I must see about jailers and check up Grubb's accounts. If there is anything to report, leave word at Tomlinson's."

Deuce got up. "Let's eat, Ace. We got the jump on Joe anyway. We do our reportin' at the Tumblin' T. I wish I knowed how to play a gui-tar!"

Joe grinned. "Eef I'm mean *hombre,* I'm tich you. No matter how good you play, w'en you seeng the *señorita* weel theenk the stray cat ees bus' loose."

As they passed out of the courthouse June Tomlinson sprang from a buckboard she had just driven up to the hitching rack and hurried toward them, her violet eyes shining.

"Hello, Mr. Sheriff! Congratulations! The Cleanup Party couldn't have picked a better candidate. And these gentlemen, I suppose, are your deputies. Oh, but aren't we going to have law and order!"

Before the "gentlemen" could answer, Dick Markley came up. Brushing past them he seized the girl's hand, head bare, that winning smile on his handsome face. "I'm shore glad you came in," he told her. "And you're not drivin' back until you've had dinner with me."

The girl colored slightly. "Why—I hadn't intended to remain in town, but if you insist—" She turned and smiled at Bob. "Your friend has such a persuasive way about him that one just can't say no. Come out to see father when you can, Bob. He likes you immensely."

Bob promised an early visit, then slowly followed

as the two strolled toward the hotel. As they drew opposite the entrance, Duke Haslam stepped forward and raised his hat. Dick presented him to June, and frowned slightly as the owner of the Paris bowed low over her hand. June acknowledged the introduction with her customary poise and, placing her fingers on Dick's arm, moved into the hotel. Duke turned, his eyes on the slim form of the girl, and Bob's blood boiled at sight of the covetous look which overspread his face.

Bob and his deputies ate dinner at the Paris, where Dick had secured a small table at one side of the room for June and himself. At the conclusion of the meal the two left the room immediately ahead of Bob's party, and as June turned to speak to Deuce, Pete Grubb sidled up to Dick and whispered something to him. Dick shrugged impatiently, excused himself, and hurried away.

June got into the buckboard, and as the four stood watching the rapidly vanishing vehicle a band of horsemen swept around the corner of the hotel, passing them at a fast trot. The big, black-bearded Kurt Dodd was in the lead, and riding beside him, face held rigidly to the front, was Dick Markley.

Deuce swore. "What's he doin' with Dodd's outfit?"

Ace flashed him a significant glance. "Mebbe Dick is just headin' in the same direction as Kurt." His voice, however, lacked conviction.

Bob said nothing. Dick was his friend, and to assume that he had gone over to the enemy was unthinkable. There was, no doubt, some good explanation of Markley's conduct.

When his deputies had departed on their assignments, Bob set about the difficult task of identifying the man who had shot John Rutherford. Painstakingly he moved from saloon to store, buying drinks and tobacco and asking casual questions. He met with no success until he reached a little *cantina* in the Mexican quarter. Here the proprietor remembered that the fellow had come into his place shortly before the fatal shooting and had bought several drinks of *tequila*. Another man had accompanied him. The proprietor knew neither of them, but the fellow's companion was short and chunky, with red hair and a freckled face. He wore a much soiled but elaborate calfskin vest.

From place to place Bob moved seeking a line on this second man. Nobody else seemed to have noticed him, and by the time he had combed the town it was supper time. He returned to the hotel, washed up, and went into the dining room. Pop Purvis, the retired cattleman, waved him to an adjoining seat.

"Ain't seen you before to congratulate you. You shore have bit off a big chunk of grief for yoreself, but I'm thinkin' you'll come through, especially with them other four hellions to help. High, low, jack, and game, and the joker. That's a great combination, boy."

"Joker?" Bob caught the allusion to the other four points but this reference to the joker puzzled him.

"Dick Markley. I seen him ride outa town with Kurt Dodd. That's a smart idee, son: to plant him on the Kady."

Bob grinned. If folks thought he had sent Dick to Dodd's spread, let them continue to think it. "You're a smart article, Pop, and there isn't much that gets by you. Now I bet you are the only man in town who can tell me the name of a short, chunky fella with red hair and a loud and dirty calfskin vest."

Pop shook his head. "Nope, I cain't tell you his name, but I know who you mean. I seen him twice in town here. Once he rode in with Kurt Dodd, and another time with Kurt's foreman, Cole Bradshaw."

Bob succeeded in hiding his elation. "Thanks, Pop. By the way, I haven't seen Duke Haslam this afternoon. Wonder where he is."

"I can tell you that. He's gone to Dutch Trumbauer's spread to look at a hawss. Heard him tell the clerk."

Pop's information was for once incorrect, but that was not the fault either of Pop's hearing or of his understanding. Duke had told the clerk plainly enough that he was riding to Trumbauer's ranch, and had actually started in that direction. Once clear of the town, however, he had swung off to the river and had followed it until he felt safe in striking directly for the Kady. It was dark by the time he reached his destination.

There was nothing about the ranch itself to arouse suspicion. The cattle which dotted the range were all legitimately branded KD, and cowboys went about the business of caring for them in exactly the same manner as other cowboys on other ranches; but as Duke approached the corrals a rider loomed up out of the darkness to challenge him. The guard carried a ready rifle.

Duke answered the challenge and the horseman

wheeled and melted into the shadows. Haslam rode to the house, dismounted, and tied his horse.

"Go right in, Duke," came a voice from the veranda. A cigarette end glowed momentarily, and Duke knew that although he had not seen the guard he had been under observation ever since passing the corrals.

He walked into the front room to find three men playing poker at a table which was illuminated by a ship's lantern swung overhead. One of the men was Kurt Dodd; the second was his foreman, Cole Bradshaw; the third was Dick Markley. All three looked up as Haslam entered.

"Hello, boys," Duke saluted them. "I haven't much time. Put down your hands and listen. I came out here to talk because I didn't want to be seen with you in town. With this seven-up combination in office we must watch our step."

"Seven-up?" frowned Dodd.

Duke explained. "That old fossil, Pop Purvis, started it. Calls that Ace fellow high, the little one low, Bob Lee jack, and the greaser game." He looked at Dick. "You're the joker."

"What have I to do with it?"

"Well, as the joker you are more or less an uncertain quantity. The set-up is favorable to us. Our game is to keep folks guessing. That is why I want you in our little company." He smiled sardonically at the frowning Markley. "You see, boys, Dick is in love."

"Cut that out!" cried Dick sharply.

Haslam's eyebrows went up. "Oh, there is nothing to be offended about. Miss Tomlinson is a wonderful young woman; you should be proud to admit that you care for her." He addressed the other two. "Unfortunately, Dick finds that he is in no position financially to court the young lady, so I have decided to provide a little nest egg for him provided he throws in with us and helps us in certain enterprises."

"What is it you want me to do?" asked Dick tightly.

Haslam leaned back in his chair and gazed at the young man through half closed lids. "Not much. The new sheriff is a bosom friend of yours; he trusts you and believes in you. That you should oppose him is unthinkable—to him. I want you to convince Lee that Kurt is running a perfectly legitimate ranch, and that he must look elsewhere for the gang which is operating in this county. You will also assist us from time to time, just as an assurance of your loyalty."

Dick swore heatedly. "I won't do it. Bob Lee is my friend."

"Friendship and business do not mix. If you elect to do this you will receive at the end of the year a fair share of the profits. I should say that your cut will amount to at least ten thousand dollars."

"Ten thousand dollars!" Dick gasped. He stared at Haslam, moistening his lips. "Ten thousand dollars," he repeated dazedly.

Haslam produced a fat wallet, opened it, and took out a wad of bills.

"As a mark of good faith I am prepared to advance you one thousand in cash before you lift a finger." He counted out some bills, replaced the wallet in his pocket, and riffled the edges of the banknotes between his fingers. "How about it?"

Dick was staring at the money as though fascinated. "Haslam, you got no right to tempt me! Bob and me have been buddies ever since he came here from Texas. He's stood by me when I hadn't a friend in the world. He's looked after me and took care of me. I—I just cain't do it."

Haslam sighed and reached for the wallet. "Very well. I won't attempt to influence your decision. But it is too bad. A thousand dollars is a lot of money. And ten thousand—" He riffled the bills again, carelessly.

Dick leaned forward and snatched the bills from his hand.

"You devil! You knew I'd fall for it. I'll do yore work for a year; not a day longer. Then I'm free. You understand? I'm free!"

"Of course. Now you're acting sensibly." He took a slip of paper from the wallet and spread it on the table. "Kurt, get me a pen. I want Dick to sign this receipt. Something I always require, Dick. I'm operating a big business, and I must keep the records straight."

Dick hastily signed at the place indicated, giving such a vicious twist to the pen at the end of the signature that the ink splattered the paper. The three observers exchanged glances. Kurt and Bradshaw were smiling thinly.

"And now," said Haslam, "to business. Here's the layout: With this new sheriff on the job the so-called Cleanup Party is looking for quick action. Well, we'll give it to them. We'll strike swiftly at first one point and then another. We'll run them dizzy; make monkeys of them.

"First we'll raid Tomlinson's spread. He has some fine three-year-olds. And the Tumbling T will work over into an excellent Diamond Cross."

"That's rubbin' it in," protested Dick. "Keep off that spread."

Duke eyed him coldly. "From now on I give the orders. You're a member of the outfit, and do as I say. It won't break Tomlinson by any means; the raid is merely intended to embarrass the sheriff. Bradshaw, you pick the boys and see that Dick has a place. Kurt, you spend the night in town. That will alibi you and make Dick's job easier when he tells Lee that your crew is innocent. We'll pull it off tomorrow night. I guess that's all."

Bradshaw winked and got to his feet, yawning. "Well, I'll hit the hay. Come on, Dick; I'll find you a bunk. And I got a money belt I'll lend you to tote that *dinero* around in. So long, Duke." He led the way from the room, Dick at his heels.

Kurt Dodd spoke drily. "Help comes high nowadays. Ten thousand dollars, with one thousand in advance. Duke, are you loco?"

Haslam grinned at him. "The other nine are to be paid at the end of the year; don't forget that. At the *end* of the year."

"Shore; I got you. But just the same is it worth even a thousand?"

"It's worth every bit of that, Kurt. You don't catch the full significance of the deal. There is a woman in it. June Tomlinson. I've taken quite a fancy to her, Kurt."

Dodd's face sobered. "Better watch yore step, Duke.

Don't go gettin' no female mixed up in this or you'll cook yore own goose."

"I'm a wealthy man," mused Haslam. "I'm right in my prime and I'm not at all repulsive. But Dick Markley and Bob Lee have the things which I lack. They have youth, fire, and enthusiasm. I'm a cold-blooded cuss; I can't rush in and sweep the damsel off her feet. Dick is madly in love with her, and I believe Lee is too, although he tries to hide it, chiefly on Dick's account. The girl has known them only a short time, but I can see that she likes them both very much. So much, in fact, that if one were to kill the other—Well, do you get my drift?"

Kurt was grinning again. "Yeah, I get you, you slippery old sidewinder! If one kills the other, it finishes both with the girl."

"And leaves the way clear for me," finished Haslam. He got up. "I'll be going, Kurt. Good night, and good luck."

CHAPTER V

HOOFPRINTS

D EUCE LOWERY pushed back his plate with a sigh of contentment. "I just cain't eat another mouthful, Miss June. Never before have I wrapped myself such a han'some repast. I've done reached the satcheration point."

"That goes double for me," echoed Ace. "Man and boy I've et from tin cans, chuck wagons, hash houses, and hotels for twenty-five years, and I ain't never enjoyed my victuals so much."

June Tomlinson smiled across the table at them. "You flatter me."

"Flatter!" cried Deuce reproachfully. "Why, ma'am, there ain't words enough for me to tell you everything I'd like to." He glanced at her meaningly, then blushed and looked away as Ace bent a hard gaze on him. "You know," he went on sadly, "it's awful tough for a man to go through life alone, with no comfortin' hand of woman to soothe his brow and mix his biscuits."

June's eyes were sparkling. "It must be terrible! But a good-looking man like you should not be bothered in that way any longer than he chooses. There are any number of nice girls who would be glad to do the soothing and the mixing."

Deuce shook his head. "I reckon I'm too partic'lar,

ma'am. Up till last week I never seen one that I'd look at a second time."

"Seems to me you looked more than once at that waitress in the Elite Cafe," said Ace tartly.

Deuce blushed. "Aw, that was just a passin' fancy."

"Yeah? And how about that little *señorita* down at Juarez; and that widder woman in Santone you met through the mattermonial agency."

"I was deceived in that widder," Deuce protested, highly uncomfortable. "The ad said she was little and had a fat income; instead it was the income that was little and her that was fat."

Ace turned to June. "You cain't believe a word he says, ma'am. He's a reg'lar Don John with wimmen. Me, I'm different. I'm steady and reliable. I ain't so long on looks, but—"

"You shore are long on everything else," Deuce interrupted. "You're so long that a lady would break her neck tryin' to look you in the face."

"And you're so short she'd get humpbacked kissin' you good-by!" Ace retorted. "A woman likes somebody who is tall enough to sweep her off her feet. I'll leave it to Miss June if she don't."

"The subject is too deep for me," June told them merrily. "Let's go into the living room and put it up to father."

They joined Tomlinson, who, because of the splints on his leg, spent most of his time in an armchair, and for an hour or so amused him with their friendly bickerings. It was dark when they took their leave to patrol the range in accordance with Bob's instructions. For awhile they rode in silence, then Ace said:

"That shore is some li'l' woman, Deuce."

"Yeah. And you hadda go blab about that waitress and widder woman. And you deceived her about yore age. Man and boy you've been eatin' for twenty-five years! Accordin' to that you didn't begin to eat until you was twelve. And that taffy about bein' steady and reliable! You should 'a' said dumb and incapable."

"Trouble with you is you're jealous."

Deuce bristled. "Jealous! Who, me? My gosh! Why, you long-legged giraffe, you're so high in the air Miss June couldn't see you with a telescope."

"And you're so low down she'd need a mikerscope to find you." A short silence; then, "Deuce, I reckon we're a pair of fools."

Deuce sighed heavily. "Ace, I reckon you're right!"

They crossed the creek which wound through the valley, continued for several miles, then, after smoking a cigarette together, separated. Deuce turned northwest, following the line of the creek, and Ace turned southeast. On Deuce's right and to Ace's left was the boundary of Kurt Dodd's Kady, which extended back into the hills on that side of the valley. In time, Deuce would reach the Big 4 of Frank Enright, the cattleman who had superintended at the hanging, and Ace would find himself on Dutch Trumbauer's Candlestick.

Deuce rode slowly, holding his cigarette so that the glowing tip was hidden in a cupped palm. Around him were cattle, some grazing, others lying down. By the time he reached the Big 4, the moon was shining, and Deuce kept as much as was possible to low spots in the range.

Halfway across the Big 4 he pulled up, dismounted

to stretch, and, grounding the reins, smoked another cigarette. Presently he remounted, turned, and started back over his beat, this time cutting closer to the Kady boundary.

At the extreme corner of Tomlinson's Tumbling T was a large spring, the overflow of which nourished a particularly lush area of grass. Here he found congregated more than the usual number of cattle. Deuce frowned at their proximity to the Kady and the concealing hills beyond, but the animals were quietly grazing or sleeping, and he rode on.

Back near the point where they had separated he met Ace, also on the return trick. They stopped and talked awhile, lounging in their saddles, then again parted, each to cover the territory over which the other had just passed. Deuce glanced at the moon and judged it to be about two o'clock. An hour later he was on Trumbauer's spread and drew rein to roll another smoke. He was twisting the end of the paper when the distant boom of a sixgun reached him.

He arrested all motion and sat erect, listening. It came again, dulled by distance. He dropped the cigarette, wheeled his horse, and jumped him into a fast run.

Back across the Tumbling T he sped, headed for the spring in the north corner. The sound of any additional gunfire was smothered beneath the pound of hoofs. For an hour he rode, then saw on the crest of a ridge a number of cattle, running from the direction of the spring. Presently he encountered another small bunch which scattered wildly at his approach.

He found the pasture at the spring silent and deserted. Drawing up to breathe his horse, he sat the saddle with ears cocked for a tell-tale sound. There was none.

Deuce swore worriedly. To attempt tracking by moonlight was foolish. He rode slowly toward the Kady, crossed the boundary and circled. From the total absence of cattle in the vicinity he judged that there must have been considerable shooting; but he came across no riderless horse, no sign whatever of the fight Ace must have precipitated.

Riding back to the spring, he slipped the bit so his horse could graze, and, squatting on the ground, set about the task of building another cigarette. He smoked it slowly, rolled and smoked another, and then a third. The moon sank lower, the sky in the east began to brighten. Deuce got to his feet, caught the horse, and adjusted the bit once more.

"Be light soon," he told the animal; then stiffened as a faint sound came to him. Somewhere on the Kady an iron-shod hoof had struck a rock.

He drew the Winchester from its sheath and levered a shell into the chamber. The sound of hoofbeats was quite plain now. Deuce's eyes narrowed and he clamped his jaws tight in his eagerness. The vague form of a horseman materialized out of the gloom, approaching at a swinging lope. Deuce raised the Winchester, steadying it over the saddle, Another fifty feet—

He swore, half in disgust, half in relief, and pushed the rifle back into the boot. "This way, Legs!" he shouted.

Ace swerved his mount slightly, pulled up within a

half dozen feet of Deuce, and, curling a long leg about the saddle horn, reached for the makings.

"About time you showed up," he said.

"Why, you dawggone—" Deuce began, then, realizing that Ace was baiting him, smothered the outburst. "Where are the prisoners?" he inquired calmly.

"That's what I was fixin' to ask you. You must of rode right past the rustlers without seein' them. They was right busy when I got here. One seen me crossin' a ridge and fired a warnin' shot."

"Too bad he didn't hit you," growled Deuce. "Ain't you got no sense, crossin' a ridge on a moonlit night?"

"I couldn't move the danged thing outa the way, could I? Or mebbe you figger I should have dug a tunnel. Anyhow, they skeedaddled and I chased 'em. Followed 'em to the hills where they split. But they was in such a hurry that they shore didn't drive any beef along with them."

"Well, let's find Bob. Those tracks will keep for a few hours."

It was daylight when they reached the Tumbling T ranch house. Deuce stopped only long enough to notify Tomlinson, who immediately ordered his crew to the spring. Reluctantly declining June's invitation to breakfast, Deuce continued to town, leaving Ace to direct Tomlinson's punchers.

Deuce found Bob in the sheriff's office, and tersely reported.

"I'll go out there at once," Bob told him. "You stay in town in my place. Get yoreself some breakfast, and if you want to sleep there's a cot in the office here. Turn in when you feel like it. So long."

He rode swiftly out of town, reaching the Tumbling T in an hour and a half. As he swung into the yard he noticed a familiar horse in the corral, and consequently was not surprised to find Dick Markley in the living room talking with Tomlinson and June.

"Howdy, folks," Bob greeted them. "Mr. Tomlinson, I dropped in to find out if yore men had reported yet."

"They're still out there, Bob. I shore hope they round up the thieves. They're Texas men, and they'll know how to deal with them."

"Then I'll be ridin'. See you later."

Dick followed him from the room. "Mind if I jog along?" he asked.

"Glad to have you, partner! Wish you were ridin' with me steady."

It was mid-morning when they reached the spring. Cattle had drifted back to the place, almost obliterating the tracks left by the raiders. Bob, however, dismounted and studied those he could find. For a few minutes he stood looking about, studying the ground and the surrounding scrub growth; then Dick saw him stiffen alertly and walk to a point some fifteen feet away. He stopped, glanced keenly at the ground, then bent over and retrieved an object which glinted in the sunlight. He was frowning thoughtfully when he returned to where Dick was lounging in his saddle.

"That's funny," he said, handing the object to Dick. "I thought you shot the only forty-one around these diggin's, but I was wrong. Somebody in the rustler outfit uses one too."

Dick took the empty cartridge and examined it with

as much evident interest as Bob had displayed. "That's right," he agreed. "Wonder who it is?"

Bob remounted and led the way from the spring, angling across the Kady in the direction taken by Tomlinson's men. The terrain became more broken as they penetrated into the hills, and they were finally compelled to slow their horses' gait to a walk.

"Shore is fine country for a rustler hideout," observed Bob.

"Still thinkin' of Kurt Dodd?"

Bob nodded somberly. "Yes. The more I study over the thing the more convinced I am that he is behind this stealin'. Dick, why did you ever sign on with that outfit?"

"Well, Bob, I'll tell you." For a few seconds Dick rode in silence. The time had come when he must carry out his odious bargain with Duke Haslam, and the task was proving harder than he had anticipated. Never before had he deliberately lied to Bob, and the knowledge that his friend would accept his word unhesitatingly made it particularly difficult to do so now.

"I signed up with Dodd thinkin' I might help you. I knew you suspected him, and if you were wrong I know you'd waste a lot of time tryin' to prove somethin' on him instead of lookin' elsewhere. Bob, Kurt got nothin' to do with this. Take last night; he said he was goin' to stay in town. Did he?"

"He did; and while he might have slipped out to the spring he never would have had time to get back again for breakfast. Kid, did you really do that for me?"

"Yeah, I did." Dick did not look at his friend, for

he knew Bob's face was alight with pleasure. In that moment Dick mentally cursed Duke Haslam and his own weak self.

Bob edged his horse over beside him and thumped him resoundingly on the back. "You old horse thief! I wondered why you didn't take that deputy job. A hundred a month is nothin' to sneeze at. And you passed it up for forty a month figurin' you would save me a little trouble! Doggone you, kid, I could lick you for that!"

"Aw, shut up," growled Dick. "I—hell! I didn't want that deputy job nohow. I ain't fit for it."

"Why, you're talkin' like a crazy man! There's nothin' I'd like better in the world than to have you sidin' me! Kid, come in with me. We'll clean up Lariat and show Duke Haslam how to run a county. What you say?"

Dick's face was tight. "I cain't do it," he said shortly. "I've passed my word. I got to stick. I tell you I've got to stick!"

"I'm sorry, kid." Bob was a bit puzzled at Dick's vehemence. "But remember, when you're free the job will be waitin' for you. Any time, partner. Savvy?"

"Yes." Dick's voice was dead. "Hell! Let's ride." He spurred his horse, disregarding the treacherous going, and for awhile set a pace which taxed Bob's mount to the utmost. Presently Dick pulled up. "Trail splits here. Which way?"

Bob studied the ground. They had been following several sets of tracks, now at the conjunction of two arroyos the trail divided. He made a random choice. "To the right; one is as good as another."

They proceeded at a more sedate pace, riding in silence. Dick was morose; Bob tranquil. Lee had Dick's explanation, and it satisfied and gladdened him. Good old Dick! Might have known he would never go over to the enemy without good cause.

The sun climbed high overhead, the heat from its rays reflected by hard packed soil and barren rock. The country was so rough as to be almost impassable, and finally Dick reined in.

"Bob, there's no use of goin' any farther. Let's turn back."

"It is pretty rough," admitted Bob, "but we'll stick to it a bit longer. Somebody came in here, and where they can go we can follow."

He drew up sharply as the sound of iron on stone came to them from beyond a bend in the arroyo. His hand fell to the gun at his hip, then dropped as Ace came into view. The tall puncher halted at sight of them, then rode slowly forward, his eyes on Dick.

"Hello, Ace," said Markley calmly.

"Howdy, Dick." Ace's eyes shifted to Bob. "I'm glad you happened along. I found somethin' back here a ways that I want to show you." He reined his horse about and waited for them to join him.

"I found somethin' too," Bob said, and passed over the empty shell. "Some one besides Dick shoots a forty-one. Found it at the spring. One of the rustlers must have taken time to reload before you set 'em in motion."

Ace examined the shell and returned it without comment, but his jaw muscles were set and his eyes narrow.

At the end of a half hour's ride the arroyo debouched

in a little green basin where the lush grass was watered by a flowing spring. "Right over there," Ace said shortly, and found a pretext to fall slightly to the rear of Dick as they crossed to the place indicated.

Bob halted his horse and looked down on the blackened embers of a fire.

"There's a corral back in them trees," Ace told him. "I figger somebody's been brandin' stock in here right recent. Over by the spring is a set of tracks I want you to look at." He sat his saddle still a bit to the rear of Dick, and his right hand lay on his thigh within inches of his sixgun.

Bob dismounted and crossed to the spring. The prints showed distinctly in the damp earth. He frowned and turned toward the two watching men. Passing behind Dick's horse, he glanced at the tracks just made by that animal.

Dick suddenly exclaimed aloud and smacked hand on leg. "I got it! They are my tracks. I remember this place now. I was here yesterday lookin' for strays. But that fire wasn't here, and I didn't see any corral. . . . Well, Bob, I'd better be gettin' back to the Kady. After all, I'm drawin' pay from Kurt Dodd for workin' cattle. So long. Hope you catch the rustlers."

"So long, Dick. Remember what I told you about that job."

Ace raised an arm in farewell, but did not speak. When Markley had disappeared from view, he swung to the ground and carefully scanned a single plain track a few feet from the branding fire.

"What is it?" Bob asked curiously.

Ace got to his feet, managing as he did so to obliter-

ate the print with one big foot. "Nothin'," he said
carelessly. "Just another track."

"You know," Bob told him, "Dick joined up with
Dodd just to find out whether or not he is behind these
doin's."

"Uh-huh," answered Ace. He was a bit shaken. Dick
had said the fire was not there the day before, and
Dick had lied. For the wind had blown some ashes
over the spot Ace had studied, and the hoof of Dick's
horse had ground those ashes into the earth.

Chapter VI

IN THE HILLS

B OB rode to the trees indicated by Ace and looked at the pole corral. There was evidence that the little inclosure had been recently occupied.

"It's my idea," said Ace, "that there was stock in this basin until a few hours ago. The rustlers had plenty time to drive it out."

"Where are Tomlinson's men?"

"Scattered all over. My gosh, Bob, you got no idea how the trails back here criss-cross. I betcha there's a hundred parks like this scattered where you cain't find them except by stumblin' over them."

"Well, let's stumble over some."

They found a trail leading from the corral and followed it. For several miles it twisted through arroyo and gully, then quite suddenly the riders found themselves in a rocky depression where the tracks disappeared completely. They circled the basin, stopping at each debouching wash to study the ground. All the passages showed tracks of some kind.

"You follow this one," Bob directed, pointing to a trail which was comparatively fresh. "I'll take another. If you don't find anything in an hour, come back and meet me here."

Ace urged his horse along the trail he had been told

to follow, and Bob retraced his course to the line of tracks they had just passed. The trail entered a shallow wash, following its convolutions deeper into the hills. Gradually the gully deepened into a gorge with rocky, scrub-covered walls, occasionally pierced by lateral passages, the bed of each marked with some kind of horse or cattle tracks.

"Looks like they are tryin' to draw me from the gorge," mused Bob. "So I reckon I'll just stick to it."

The trail ahead of him became increasingly difficult of passage, and finally the last faint hoofprints vanished altogether. Bob, however, pressed doggedly on, reasoning that the very absence of tracks might have been calculated to discourage his keeping up the gorge. A half hour later he was elated to find the going less difficult; the trail widened and slanted downward in an easy gradient that his horse welcomed with a grunt of relief. Quite abruptly he rounded a bend to find the gorge widening into another mountain park. Cattle grazed placidly in the near distance, and off to his right, among a cluster of oaks, was a small cabin. In the doorway,, smoking, sat a man.

The man did not rise at Bob's approach, but Lee caught a flash of movement in the trees and had a fleeting glimpse of a running figure before it was completely hidden by the scrub. As he drew near the shack his blood quickened and he peered narrowly at the one who sat so calmly drawing on his pipe. He had seen at once that the fellow was red-headed; now he noticed that he wore an ornate but dirty calfskin vest, and Bob knew he was looking at the person who had been in the company of John Rutherford's murderer.

Twenty feet from the cabin he drew rein. The red-headed fellow removed his pipe and growled, "Whadda you want?"

"You," answered Bob, and drew his gun.

The fellow stared at him apparently undisturbed. "If this is a holdup you've shore got the wrong party."

"It's a holdup, all right." Watching alertly, he swung from the saddle. "I'm the sheriff. Maybe you saw me in Lariat the night before election. You know—the night they hanged yore buddy for shootin' John Rutherford."

"I ain't been in Lariat for months."

"You were seen in a *cantina* with the jigger who killed Rutherford." Bob reached for the handcuffs he carried in a hip pocket. "Stick out yore hands."

At sight of the irons the fellow came to his feet, eyes blazing. "By Godfrey, no! What right you got to arrest me?"

"Accessory before the fact; suspicion; spittin' on the sidewalk; anything."

"I tell you I wasn't in Lariat that night!"

"Manuel Gonzales said you were, and I'm goin' to give him a chance to identify you."

The man glared at him, freckled face red with anger. "You shore got yore nerve!" he choked.

"Stick out yore paws."

Disregarding the drawn Colt, the fellow sprang at him, an incoherent growl rumbling from his throat. His huge hairy hands were extended, his red-lidded eyes blazed wrathfully.

Bob did not fire, for should he kill the fellow a possible link in the chain which was to connect Duke

Haslam with the slaying would be broken. He aimed a swift blow at the fellow's head, but a wide-flung arm warded off the gun barrel, and the next instant they were locked in each other's arms.

The man was short but powerful. Bob grunted as the fellow's muscular arms tightened about him, squirmed desperately to avoid the tripping leg which was thrust behind him. He dropped his gun in order that his hands would be unhampered, and strained to break the hold which threatened to crack his spine.

The man's evil, sweating face was thrust close to his, the red-lidded eyes flamed venomously. Bob ducked forward, driving his forehead against the bridge of the fellow's nose. The red-head's hold slightly relaxed, and Bob succeeded in getting his forearms between himself and the man's chest. He strained outward, slipped low, and threw the fellow heavily.

The breath was knocked from the other's body, and he could do nothing but lie on his back and gasp. Bob got to his feet, found his gun and the handcuffs, and clicked the latter on the thick wrists. When the red-head had recovered his wind, Bob ordered him to his feet. "Where's yore horse?"

The man nodded toward the trees behind the cabin. "Corral," he gasped.

"All right, head for it. I'll be behind you with a gun." Leaving his horse standing, Bob followed the stocky red-head past the cabin and into the grove. He glanced into the shack as he passed and saw that it was empty.

He walked warily, for he remembered the man who had ducked into the grove as he was riding toward the cabin; nevertheless, what happened was so entirely unexpected that he was unable to prevent it.

They were approaching the corral when the man before him suddenly tripped and went down, manacled hands extended before him to break his fall. It was done so naturally that Bob had no suspicion of treachery until a flash on the far side of the corral caught his eye.

He acted immediately and almost involuntarily, dropping to the ground as a rifle whanged and a bullet cut the air directly above him. The flash Bob had caught was that of sunlight on rifle barrel, and had he not ducked instantly he would have been hit. As it was, his erstwhile prisoner having rolled to one side, Bob lay in the middle of the trail entirely exposed to the rifleman's fire.

Bob did some rolling himself, bringing up in the scrub on the opposite side of the trail. Bullets were searching him out, scattering dust, whining through the low bushes. He found a little hollow and made himself as small as was possible. He dared not even raise his arm to shoot.

Presently the firing ceased and Bob concluded that the marksman was reloading. He got to hands and knees and scurried through the scrub until he reached a tree. Circling its base he got to his feet, keeping the trunk between him and the enemy. His prisoner had vanished. Presently Bob heard the sound of hoofs and caught a brief glimpse of two men riding rapidly away.

To pursue was foolish; there were too many hiding places for one man to ferret out. He returned to the cabin and searched it, but found nothing offering a clue to the identities of the two, or, for that matter, implicating them in any wrong-doing.

Mounting, he rode into the park. All the cattle he encountered wore a large Diamond-Cross on their flanks. He roped one and examined it carefully. The brand had originally been a Big 4, and the ear marks had been completely removed by a diagonal slash. Bob marked the location of the park in his memory and retraced his way to the rocky depression. Ace had returned and was seated in the shade, smoking.

"Find anything?" he inquired as Bob rode up.

Lee related his experience. "How about you?"

"No luck. Trail petered out and I turned back. Bob, we'll have to come in here with an army if we want to run down all these tracks."

Bob squinted at the sun. "We'll run 'em down sooner or later. Right now I reckon we'd better head for the Tumblin' T if we aim to have supper there."

And at about that time, Dick Markley dropped off his horse in Lariat and sauntered into the Paris saloon. Duke Haslam was not in sight, but a bartender nodded toward a door, and Dick began moving in its direction. Presently he was leaning against its frame, and, when he was certain he was not observed, he twisted the knob, opened it far enough to squeeze through, and closed it silently behind him.

He was in Haslam's office. It was a small room between kitchen and saloon, with one window and another door opening into the hotel dining room. Dick had hardly entered when this second door opened and Haslam came in. He slipped the bolts on both doors and addressed Dick coldly.

"You should have been here long ago. What held you up?"

"Kurt didn't give me yore message until after two o'clock. I rode over to the Tumblin' T this mornin' and met Bob Lee there. You know the raid last night went haywire?"

Haslam stared at him. "What happened?"

"Well, Bradshaw took us to the north corner of the Tumblin' T and put the boys to work roundin' up. I was standin' guard. Some jigger came bustin' over the range toward us, and I fired a warnin' signal. This fella cut loose with a Winchester, and we dragged out of there."

"Who was this fellow who broke up the raid?"

"Reckon it was Ace Talbot."

"That tall deputy of Lee's? What was he doing out there?"

"I don't know, but he was Johnny-on-the-spot. Look here, Duke; are you shore you ain't underestimatin' Bob Lee? I've known him a right smart while and he shapes up pretty foxy to me."

Haslam made an impatient gesture. "I know all about him."

"Well, he's from Texas and so are his deputies. Tomlinson and his crew are from there too. We're shore fillin' up with Texas men, and I got a pretty healthy respect for them."

"I never met one yet who was bullet-proof," Haslam told him. "Get on with the yarn. What happened after he broke up the party?"

"We rode for the hills and scattered. I cut around as soon as I could and headed for the Tumblin' T.

Deuce Lowery had come in with Ace and had gone to town after Lee. When Bob came out I rode with him. Figgered you might want to know what went on. First off he found an empty shell from my gun. Showed it to me and said he reckoned somebody else besides me shot a forty-one. Then we rode up the gully together and finally he stumbled on one of Shab Cannon's parks. And at the edge of a spring he found the tracks of my horse."

"What did you tell him?"

"Said I was there the day before lookin' for strays. I buffaloed him, all right; but I know Bob Lee. He'll keep pokin' around until he does uncover somethin'."

Haslam's lips twisted in a sneer. "Then the thing to do is draw him away from the hills. The next two jobs will be around Lariat. That is why I sent for you." He crossed to the window, looked out, then came back and sat down facing Dick. "The south-bound stage is due in Lariat tomorrow at noon. That means it crosses Navajo Pass around ten. There is a gold shipment aboard. You will hold up that stage and take the money box."

Dick stared at him. "Wait a minute! You got plenty more men able to handle a job like that. Kurt or Bradshaw, for instance."

"Kurt and Bradshaw will be in town. Besides, this is part of your job to fool Lee. You won't tackle it alone. Tell Kurt to fix you up with four men and a pack-horse. It will be easy."

Dick was frowning. "I don't like it."

"I suppose not, but it's got to be done. Now listen. Put on clothes that won't be recognized—you can find some at the ranch—and ride the horse Kurt will furnish. Tie a bandana over your face, and if you have to talk be careful to disguise your voice. The climb to the top of the pass is long, and the stage team will be walking. There are plenty rocks big enough to hide you and your horse. When the stage is about to pass, ride out and cover the messenger. Have a couple of the boys come out with the pack-horse and lift the strong box. That is all. Don't bother the passengers. As soon as the stage pulls out you can beat it. Get back to the ranch, change clothes, climb on your own horse and ride over to the Tomlinsons."

Dick swore uneasily. "I tell you I don't like it, Haslam."

"Still want that other nine thousand, don't you?"

Dick continued to glower, but the fire had gone from his eyes.

Haslam spoke smoothly. "This, like last night's raid, is designed only to worry Lee. As a matter of fact, the specie is consigned to me. Nobody will suspect me of stealing my own gold; and since Kurt and Bradshaw will both be in town, even their worst enemies will have to admit that they could have had no hand in the holdup."

Dick got reluctantly to his feet. "All right; I'll do it. But, Haslam, don't figure out any more deals like this. It's not in our contract."

"No? Didn't you agree to participate in our enterprises from time to time as an evidence of good faith?"

Dick's face was grim. "Yeah; but I didn't agree to do all yore dirty work. I tell you, if it wasn't for that ten thousand dollars—"

"My dear boy, without that ten thousand dollars I wouldn't ask a thing of you. Every man has his price; yours happens to be ten thousand dollars. But you've got to earn it. . . . Go out this door and nobody will see you leave."

Dick rode slowly back toward the Kady mulling over his conversation with Duke Haslam. He began to see now the depths to which he might sink under the pressure brought to bear against him by the wily owner of the Paris. His first feeling was one of resentment, a resentment that was presently tempered by thought of the reward Haslam had dangled before his eyes.

Duke had said that every man had his price, and Duke was right. A man who would not consider a ten-thousand-dollar bribe might be bought for twenty; one who scorned twenty would sell his soul for fifty. Even Bob, Dick told himself, must have his price. Suppose Duke had riffled the edges of a thousand dollars in notes before Bob's eyes, they'd stand out on stems too. Or would they? Dick experienced a feeling of uncertainty. He shrugged it off impatiently.

"Shore he has his price," he muttered. "He'd be a fool if he didn't."

Having thus convinced himself that he was perfectly justified in doing as Duke Haslam directed, Markley fell to thinking about the contemplated holdup. In spite of his reluctance to tackle the job, his blood quickened. Once reconciled to the task he found this an adventure that appealed to his reckless spirit. He knew Navajo Pass as well as anybody; a holdup at that point would be simplicity itself. An old Stetson, a discarded coat, overalls—

His horse slackened its pace and Dick looked up. He was approaching the fork in the trail which led to the Tumbling T. After a moment's indecision Dick reined the animal into it. He wanted to see and talk with June, if only for a minute. Sleeping or awake the girl's face haunted him.

The sun had disappeared when at last he drew rein at the house hitching rack. Two horses stood at the rail, and now that he was close enough to make them out distinctly, he recognized them as belonging to Bob and Ace. The blood beat a bit faster in his veins; after all, this was like a big game, a game where he stacked his wit and resourcefulness against the keen mind of his friend. If only Bob were a bit less stanch!

As he strode across the gallery, June came to the door to welcome him. She smiled and extended her hand; Dick grasped it between both his own and pressed it. His eyes were very eager, very bold.

"Just stopped in a minute to say hello. I'm gettin' so I cain't ride by the fork in the trail without turnin' into it."

The twilight hid the delicate color which mounted to the girl's cheeks. She withdrew her hand hastily. "Come in, Dick; supper will soon be ready."

"I shouldn't," he told her. "I'm supposed to be workin' for the Kady."

She looked at him frankly. "I wish you weren't; I wish you were working for us. Why don't you talk to father about it? I'm sure he could use another hand."

Dick's smile was a bit crooked. "I've passed my word to Kurt Dodd. Don't tempt me."

"I believe Dodd is a rascal," she said bluntly. "He's your boss, and you wouldn't admit it even if you knew it to be true; but I believe it just the same. I wish you would work for the Tomlinsons."

"I'm workin' for one of them every day of the week, and when I make my pile I'll have somethin' to say to her."

June turned quickly away. "Come in," she invited.

Bob and Ace were in the living room talking with Tomlinson. As Dick entered, Ace's face went hard; but Bob turned to him with a smile.

"Hello, Dick. Glad you dropped in. You don't happen to know a short, husky red-headed chap who wears a dirty calfskin vest, do you?"

Dick shook his head. "Cain't say that I do. Why?"

Bob told him of the encounter in the hills which had culminated in the escape of his prisoner and the finding of the rustled stock.

Dick listened gravely. "There are a lot of parks back there."

"Too bad they're so close to Kurt Dodd's spread," said Ace. "Some evil-minded folks will be suspectin' him."

"If you suspect Kurt, you're wrong. I told Bob he had nothin' to do with this rustlin'."

"You been ridin' for him two days and you know him that well?"

"I don't have to ride with a man forever to find out the color of his hair."

June interrupted the conversation to announce supper. Dick refused her invitation to stay. "I got work to do on the Kady," he said.

She saw him to the door, and for another moment he held her hand between both his own. "Good night," he said softly. "You'll be seein' me again, soon."

"Dick, I wish you'd leave that spread."

He laughed grimly and released her hand. "You're as bad as Bob and Ace. I tell you Kurt Dodd is all right. I know what I'm doin'. Good night."

He swung into his saddle and rode swiftly toward the Kady. June Tomlinson stood watching his erect form until it was swallowed by the dusk; then, with a worried sigh, turned and went into the house.

CHAPTER VII

SEEDS OF SUSPICION

THE supper was thoroughly appreciated by Bob and Ace. The former was in good spirits, for while he knew that this was but the beginning, he could not underestimate the damage to the prestige of the rustler gang in so completely frustrating their first coup under the new administration.

Ace, on the other hand, was morose. Never one to talk much, he was more taciturn than ever. The discovery of the horse track in the mountain park would have meant nothing had Dick not chosen to lie about it. If he had, as he said, been looking for strays the day before, there could have been no reason for denying the presence of the branding fire. By stating that he had not seen it he had cast a doubt in Ace's mind as to the errand which had really taken him to the park.

What worried the tall puncher was the fact that he could not bring himself to confide his suspicions to Bob. On the impulse of the moment he had destroyed the tell-tale print in order to spare Bob the pain of finding Dick disloyal; but if Markley permitted the evidence against him to accumulate, sooner or later Bob could not fail to realize the truth.

Ace noticed June's clouded brow when she joined

85

them at the table, and wondered just how much she suspected. June Tomlinson was a very discerning young woman, and she appeared to be more than ordinarily interested in Dick. If Markley had chosen the crooked path his defection would hurt more than one person.

They repaired to the living room after the meal was finished, and while Ace talked with Tomlinson, June found occasion to speak to Bob. She came directly to the point.

"Knowing what friends you are, I've been wondering why Dick hasn't been appointed a deputy. Or is that an official secret?"

Bob smiled. "Dick doesn't care for that kind of work. He wouldn't want to be tied down by legal restrictions."

"I hate to see him riding for Kurt Dodd. I don't know Dodd personally, but one is bound to pick up gossip, and that raid right on the border of his spread is rather significant."

Bob nodded. "I know. But Kurt was in town while that raid was bein' pulled. He would have had no hand in it."

"His being in town might have been a blind. That foreman of his, Bradshaw, is probably as great a villain as is Dodd. He wasn't in town, was he?"

"No-o, he wasn't." Bob regarded the girl gravely. "Reckon I'd better set yore mind at ease, Miss June. Dick joined up with Dodd in order to find out whether or not Kurt's men are in this business."

Her face brightened. "You sent him?"

"Well—no; not exactly. It was Dick's idea. You see, we've been pretty good friends for a long while. Dick figured that I would camp on Dodd's trail tryin' to get somethin' on him, so he joined the Kady to learn for himself. He told me that as far as he could determine Kurt Dodd is runnin' a legitimate ranch."

The girl was eyeing him thoughtfully. "And what do you think?"

"I don't know. Dick wouldn't lie to me. If he is mistaken, it is because he himself has been deceived. Knowin' how friendly we are it stands to reason that Dodd would hide his crookedness from him. Since meetin' that red-head this mornin', though, I'm almost ready to leave Dodd out of it."

"Why?"

"Well, this red-head had a cabin in a park full of stolen cattle. There may be a gang under his leadership workin' in the hills and stealin' from the valley ranchers, Dodd included."

"Didn't you tell father that this red-headed man was seen in town twice, once with Kurt Dodd and again with Bradshaw?"

"I reckon I did. I don't know what to think, Miss June. I'm keepin' an open mind for the present. But Dick's square; I'd bet my bottom dollar on that. He's a fine, upstandin' boy. You will never regret knowin' him."

June spoke very quietly. "You think a lot of him, don't you?"

"We've been friends a long time," he repeated.

"I like him too. I would love to help him. He is the kind that needs help: wild, impulsive, perhaps a bit weak. One of those likable chaps who are apt to do things on the spur of the moment and then regret them later. I don't want to see him go wrong, but if he is mixed up with this Dodd outfit, and if Kurt is the kind of man we think he is, I'm afraid for the boy."

"It's kind of you to want to help him," Bob said soberly. "Dick doesn't remember his mother and he has no brothers or sisters. Reckon that's why I sort of cottoned to him. He thinks a heap of you, Miss June; maybe if you talked with him he'd quit the Kady."

"I have spoken to him. I urged him to ask father for a job. He told me he had passed his word to Dodd."

Bob smiled at her. "Dick is his own master and knows what he is about. If he finds that Dodd is not on the square, he'll quit."

And there they left it. But Bob wondered as he rode to Lariat whether Dick realized how lucky he was in having such a stanch friend in June Tomlinson, and June wondered as she stood on the veranda gazing after him, whether Dick fully appreciated the fine loyalty of this clear-eyed Texan.

Bob reached Lariat around ten o'clock, found Deuce in the sheriff's office and sent him out to join Ace. It was not likely that the rustlers would strike again immediately, but Bob was taking no chances.

He stabled his horse and entered the Paris. Dutch Trumbauer and Frank Enright were there, and he drew them to one side. Neither had heard of the raid on the Tumbling T. Bob told them about it, and set them to staring.

"Py golly!" exclaimed Dutch. "Dey are beginning it already yet!"

"Yeah," agreed Enright, "but they got no farther

than the beginnin'; remember that, Dutchy. It does a man good to know that at last we got a go-get-'em sheriff and deputies in office! Bob, just breakin' up that raid hurt them more than you realize. It should be advertised all over the county. No matter if you didn't get any of them, it's their first set-back, and you shore gave them somethin' to think about."

"Dot iss right," agreed Trumbauer. "Dey haf found dot dey can't pust in and run stock out yet venever dey like. Soon dey find dot with high, low, chack, and der game in von hand against dem, dey can't so frisky get."

"Do either of you know a short, chunky red-headed jasper who sports a dirty calfskin vest?" asked Bob.

The two cattlemen eyed each other, then shook their heads. "Nobody around these diggin's that fits that description," said Enright. "Why?"

"Manuel Gonzales said such a man came into his *cantina* on election eve with the fella who later shot Rutherford. Nobody seems to know him. I ran across him in the hills today. He was sittin' in the doorway of a cabin in a park full of cattle. I put the cuffs on him to bring him in, but a partner of his opened up with a Winchester, and he got away. I looked at the cattle. Enright, your Big 4 had been changed to a Diamond-Cross."

"By Judas!" swore Enright. "I'll get the boys together in the mornin' and we'll comb those hills."

"I'd rather you didn't," said Bob slowly. "Cleanin' up will be a big job, Frank. I wish you'd do me the favor of keepin' what I've told you to yoreself until later. When we go in there we'll land with a crash that will put the fear of the Almighty in a few hearts, but the time isn't ripe."

Enright frowned. "And I sit back and twiddle my thumbs while they steal me blind, eh?"

"If necessary, yes. Remember we're workin' against an organized gang. This isn't a bunch of common thieves; they have brains behind them."

Trumbauer snorted scornfully. "Kurt Dodd? Pah! He iss not the brains of a shicken got."

"I didn't say it was Dodd. But I have a hunch that you can look for the lightning to strike again, and strike soon."

"Well, you're the doctor," said Enright. "I'll keep quiet until you say the word."

On the way out, Duke Haslam stopped Bob. "Heard you had a little trouble out at the Tumbling T last night."

Bob turned on him swiftly. "How did you find that out?"

Haslam smiled and shrugged. "I don't miss much. News like that is bound to get around, you know."

Bob continued his way through the swinging doors. He was wondering how Haslam had heard about the raid. He had told only Enright and Trumbauer. On an impulse he mounted to the hotel veranda and dropped into a chair beside Pop Purvis. If by any chance Deuce had mentioned the matter Pop would be sure to have heard it.

"Howdy, Bob," greeted the old cattleman. "How goes the sheriffin'?"

"So-so," replied Bob carelessly.

"Well, I reckon things will go along right smooth for

a while," said Pop; and Bob knew Deuce had not talked.

"Any strangers in town today?"

"Shucks, no. Town's dead. Nobody even rode in but you and the joker."

"Dick?"

"Yep. He come in late this evenin' and went into the saloon." Pop glanced sidewise at the man beside him. "He come out of the hotel."

"Went in the saloon and came out of the hotel? You sure of that?"

"Shore as I'm a foot high. Come out that door behind us. I was settin' right here in this chair."

"Reckon he went into the kitchen for somethin' to eat," said Bob. He got to his feet and yawned. "I'm goin' to turn in. So long, Pop."

He walked to the office, undressed, and stretched out on the cot, but he didn't go to sleep for a long time. Mentally he conjured up a picture of the interior of the Paris saloon. There was a door leading to the alley, from whence Dick could easily have made his way to the hotel kitchen. And there was another door leading into Duke Haslam's office. From the office one could enter the dining room by still another door. Which route had Dick taken?

"You're a hell of a friend!" Bob told himself savagely. "Dick's square; you know it. Why worry about it?" He dismissed the subject and gathered the blankets about him.

Early next morning, twenty miles north of Lariat, José Villegas pulled on his boots and set about preparing breakfast. After he had eaten, he cleaned up the utensils, made up his blanket roll, and led his horse to a nearby spring to drink. Then he saddled up, mounted, and headed for the road. In the scrub he halted the horse and, cocking a leg about the horn, smoked patiently.

Presently came the rattle of wheels and the clink of chain and the stage rolled by. Joe had a glimpse of driver and messenger, the latter with a shotgun across his knees, then the vehicle was hidden by the foliage. Joe waited a few minutes, then spurred onto the road and put his horse to a slow lope.

Hour after hour he rode, occasionally singing a little Spanish song just for the sake of hearing his own voice. Then he noticed that the stage team had slowed to a walk. The vehicle was ascending the grade to Navajo Pass.

Joe checked his own mount, eyes on the coach ahead. He struck the grade and pulled to a walk. The stage reached the top of the incline and gradually dropped from view except for its very top. Presently that, too, would disappear over the crest of the pass.

But it didn't! The upper part of the back remained in view, and Joe realized at last that it had stopped. It was not the habit of the driver to breathe his horses here, but it was possible that some small damage to the harness had necessitated the halt. It was also possible—

Joe spurred his horse up the grade at a run. Nearer and nearer the summit of the pass he drew, until at last the entire coach came into view. Joe noticed that the driver was sitting stiffly with his hands raised. He also saw a man with a scarf over the lower half of his face sitting a motionless horse and holding a gun extended threateningly before him, while two other men, afoot, led a pack-horse toward the vehicle.

Joe's face brightened in anticipation as he drew the Winchester from its scabbard under his leg.

The pack-horse was halted close to the stage, and one of the men climbed over the wheel to remove the strong box. Joe raised the rifle, aimed hurriedly at the bandit leader, and squeezed the trigger.

Now José was a fair enough shot with a sixgun, and the way he could handle a knife was uncanny; but with a rifle, and atop a lunging horse, he was by no means a sterling performer. The bullet aimed at the mounted man went through the head of the pack-horse, which folded up and dropped beside the coach. The effect of the shot, however, left nothing to be desired.

The man on the stage nearly broke a leg getting to the ground, and the one already there streaked for the bowlders where he had left his horse. The leader wheeled his mount and started blazing away at Joe with his sixgun, until three or four rifle slugs cut the air about his head, whereupon he gave ground and headed for the far side of the pass.

Joe reached the level on which the stage was halted, stopped long enough to ascertain that, besides the pack-horse, there had been no casualties, then spurred in pursuit. He found where five sets of tracks entered a lateral ravine, followed them swiftly from one twisting passage to another, crossed flats, mounted ridges, plunged into gullies and washes and out again.

For two hours he chased them doggedly, his face streaming with sweat, his horse lathered and laboring;

then one of the five sets of tracks swerved into another lateral. Joe stuck to the four remaining. Presently a second set led off to one side, then a third, and finally a fourth. One set continued onward, and to this Joe stuck with the persistence of a bloodhound.

The sun reached the meridian and started its westward slant. Joe's horse was almost exhausted. Then, quite suddenly, he found himself in a little mountain park with grazing cattle. On the far side of the basin he saw a cabin and a corral partly hidden by the trees.

Joe urged his flagging horse across the meadow, investigated the cabin swiftly but cautiously, found it unoccupied, and continued to the corral. Standing inside the inclosure was the outlaw leader's horse, head low, swaying on its feet. The water dripped from its heaving flanks, and a dark patch on its back testified to the recent presence of a saddle. Joe circled the corral, found a trail leading into a gorge, and followed it. He was forced to move more slowly because of the condition of his horse.

Two hours later he found himself in the valley on what he recognized as a corner of the Kady. Here the trail thinned out in the grass. Riding slowly, about a mile ahead of him, was a horseman. Joe urged his tired mount to a lope. Presently the other turned in his saddle and looked back. Joe waved, and the horseman halted, waiting for him.

As he drew closer, the Mexican's eyes narrowed and his mobile lips were compressed in a fine line. When he overtook the other, however, the tautness had vanished and he was smiling wearily.

"*Señor* Deek, I'm not look for fin' you here."

"No? Well, I work for the Kady, and I'm ridin' over to the Tumblin' T. What are you doin' around here?"

"I'm theenk I'm get los' in the heels," Joe told him. "Come; I'm go to the *rancho* weeth you."

He swung in beside Dick, who slowed his pace to a walk out of consideration for Joe's mount. The Mexican rolled a cigarette and smoked indolently, but from beneath lowered eyelids he was studying every detail of equipment on man and horse.

Bob and Ace spurred from the Tumbling T to meet them.

"I just came out from town," the former explained. "The stage got in at noon with the news, and I figured you might leave word at Tomlinson's."

"What news?" asked Dick.

"Of the holdup," Bob told him. "Five men stuck them up at the top of Navajo Pass. Joe was trailing the stage and jumped them. Any luck, Joe?"

The Mexican shrugged. "I'm follow five track through the heels. One by one they leave the trail until I'm follow a single 'orse. That 'orse I'm fin' in leetle park. I'm follow trail to the Kady. Then I fin' *Señor* Deek and we ride together. W'at luck you say I'm have?"

"Not much. Well, it's a slippery outfit, but we'll catch up with them sooner or later."

They dismounted before the Tomlinson house. June had come to the door, and Dick sprang to greet her without waiting for the others. As Bob was about to follow, the Mexican caught him by the sleeve.

"You and Ace come weeth me to the corral. I mus' spik weeth you."

They rounded a corner of the house and made for the corral in its rear. Here they halted.

"*Señor* Bob," said the Mexican, his face grave, "I'm hate lak hell to tell you thees, but you mus' know. The man w'at hold up the stage ees—Deek."

Bob jerked erect as though he had been struck. "What's that?"

Joe nodded grimly. "Ees heem. I'm follow to the park I'm tell you about. I'm fin' 'orse, and I'm fin' Deek one, two mile ahead when I reach Kady. He ees change hees 'orse and hees clothes. Also he ees wash hees face. But the saddle she ees ver' wet, and so ees hees hair. I am not meestake."

"I reckon Joe's right, Bob," said Ace. "Remember that track I was lookin' at in the park yeste'day? Well, it was made by Dick's horse. He said there was no brandin' fire there the day before, but he lied. That print of his was *over* the ashes from the fire. Bob, as shore as shootin' he's ridin' with that rustler outfit."

Bob stared at him for a moment, then swung on his heel and walked swiftly toward the house. Ace and the Mexican exchanged glances. Joe shrugged.

"Bob ees not want to believe until he fin' out for heemself."

Ace sighed. "Yeah, I know. Aw, hell! What's it all comin' to anyhow?"

CHAPTER VIII

CALAMITY

BOB paused by the hitching rack on his way to the house. He was hard hit, for to Dick he had given his entire confidence and it was difficult to believe the boy had played him false; yet the evidence of the empty forty-one cartridge combined with the positive statements made by Ace and Joe had shaken his faith to the very foundation. Had it been any other than Dick he must have been convinced at once.

Dick's horse was as fresh as a daisy, but Bob could see that the saddle had recently been stripped from a very wet animal. Bob left the rack hurriedly and started for the house as Ace and Joe rounded the corner.

He found June, her father, and Dick in the living room, and slanted a searching glance at his friend. Dick was talking gaily, and Bob decided that if he were really guilty he was very skillful at playing a part. As Joe and Ace entered, the three looked up and greetings were exchanged all around.

"Bob," said Dick, "you ought to get after yore deputies about the way they mistreat their horses. Joe has just about ridden his into the ground."

"Yore own saddle is pretty wet," said Bob tightly.

"But the horse is dry. I do change before I kill my mount."

"Been ridin' hard?"

"I'll tell a man I have. We rounded up the wildest bunch I ever tangled with. Back in the hills; strays. You work some of those draws and slopes and you'll find it takes the pepper out of a horse right now."

Bob turned to Tomlinson. "Joe has been trailin' the stage in and out of Lariat. This mornin' five bandits held it up. Joe arrived in time to save the strong box, and chased them into the hills back of the Kady."

Deuce, just awake after his morning nap, spoke from the doorway. "Good work, Joe!"

"Yeah, Joe, it shore was," said Dick carelessly. "You fellas are playin' hob with that bunch; but don't get careless. They're not used to set-backs."

June glanced at him quickly. "You should join them, Dick. With high, low, jack, game, and the joker in one hand, they wouldn't stand a chance."

Dick grinned at her. "Maybe when I convince Bob that Kurt Dodd is not in on this I will."

"Huh!" grunted Ace skeptically. "Accordin' to you, all that slab-sided boss of yores needs is a harp in his paws and a crown on his head. Any time I get to believin' that Kurt Dodd is a lily white angel I want somebody to tap me on the coco and put me out of my mis'ry."

Dick shrugged. "Where was Kurt when this holdup occurred?"

"He was in town," Bob answered. "And so was Bradshaw."

"Seems like they're gettin' the habit of bein' in

Lariat whenever anything happens," said Deuce. "It's so reg'lar it's suspicious."

Bob got to his feet. "Well, I'm ridin' back to town. Joe, you pick up the stage as usual. Ace, stick to this side of the valley. Deuce, you'd better mosey over on the other side. So long, folks."

He raised an arm in farewell and went out to his horse. His eyes fell again on the wet saddle of Dick Markley. The explanation given by his friend was entirely logical. Bob swore savagely as he swung into the saddle. It was just possible that both Ace and Joe were wrong, but he realized that his own judgment was tempered by friendship for Dick. Markley had been closer than a brother to him, and he would have trusted his life in the boy's hands.

It was late afternoon when he reached Lariat. He found the town seething. The news of the holdup had been broadcast, and men surrounded him almost before he had alighted to slap his back and congratulate him on his foresight in having the stage trailed. Both Trumbauer and Enright were in town.

"Py golly, dot vas fine!" declared Dutch. "Maybe now dey learn dot it don't pay, dis monkey-pusiness."

"You've got 'em on the run, Bob," Enright told him. "Come into the Paris and I'll buy you a drink."

Bob compromised on a cigar and finally managed to escape on the plea of official business. He went to his office, cleaned up what desk work remained, then visited the jail, which was located in the rear of the second floor of the courthouse. There were five cells, two on each side of the central corridor and one at its end, all unoccupied at the present time. The jailer had an office here, and Bob found him yawning over a solitaire layout.

"I shore wish you'd bring in some prisoners," he complained. "This doin' nothin' is the hardest work I ever run across."

"You'll make up for it presently," Bob promised.

On his way through the corridor he passed the prosecuting attorney's office. Glancing through the open doorway he beheld Thaddeus Poole and Judge Bleek absorbed in a game of chess. The county's legal machinery, with the exception of the sheriff's office, seemed utterly at a standstill.

Bob ate supper in company with Enright and Trumbauer, then spent an hour or two in a circuit of the town. He was uneasy and apprehensive for some reason or other, and even after he had gone to bed he rolled about restlessly until long after the sounds of Lariat's night life had quieted.

The same feeling persisted when he arose the next morning. He ate at the hotel, walked about town a bit, then finally returned to the office. Here he forced himself to the task of checking over Pete Grubb's records and attempting to install some sort of system for himself. By mid-morning this task was finished and he found himself at loose ends again.

The sound of hoofs took him to the window in time to see Dick Markley ride by. Bob reached for his Stetson and made his way to the street. Dick halted at the Paris hitching rack and, swinging to the ground, passed through the doorway into the saloon.

Bob continued leisurely down the street and entered the place a minute or so after Dick. For a moment he stood just within the doorway looking about. Four men sat a a table playing poker, and two more lounged against the bar. Dick was not in sight, and neither was Haslam.

Bob went outside, and, after a moment's indecision, crossed the street and entered the Cattleman's Bank. This was a low brick building with iron-barred windows and heavy door. There was a desk near the front window, and, after exchanging greetings with the teller, Bob picked up a pen and did some idle scratching on a pad of deposit slips, keeping, at the same time, an eye on the entrance to the Paris.

A half hour passed, then he saw a man in the hotel entrance and a moment later recognized Dick. Markley stood just within the lobby, looking through the doorway. Assured that he was not noticed, he strode quickly to the sidewalk and flung himself into the saddle.

Bob tossed the paper into the waste paper basket and started out the door; but Dick rode by without even glancing at him, and Bob could see that the young fellow's cheeks were flushed and his eyes glinting. He stood on the sidewalk looking after Dick until Markley disappeared from view, then shook his head worriedly and crossed the street. As he passed the saloon he glanced over the half doors. Haslam was leaning against the bar, smoking.

Noon brought the south-bound stage, and Bob walked down to the station. He watched the agent and a helper carry the strong box to the bank, the messenger strolling after them with his shotgun at the ready. The following day was pay-day, and the bank had shipped in specie to meet the cattlemen's demands.

Dinner, then a long afternoon. Towards evening June Tomlinson drove in to make some purchases, and Bob's face lighted in anticipation. The girl had been much in his thoughts, a fact which annoyed him at times because he knew Dick loved her and believed that she cared for Markley. The less he dreamed about her, he told himself, the better for his peace of mind; yet to banish her entirely from his thoughts was as impossible as to still the beating of the ocean waves.

He started toward her, but before he was anywhere near, Duke Haslam stepped out of the saloon and spoke to her. While Bob watched, they strolled away together. Later he saw them coming from a store, Haslam's arms laden with packages. Duke placed the purchases in the buckboard and helped June to the seat. Bob, remembering Haslam's expression when he had first met the girl, swore under his breath as Duke raised his forty-dollar Stetson in a farewell salute.

He ate his supper alone, the uncomfortable feeling of apprehension gripping him anew. There was trouble brewing; he could feel it in his bones just as he could detect the approach of bad weather. He made a short circuit of the town and went to bed at an early hour.

He fell asleep almost immediately, only to awake late in the night as refreshed as though it were morning. He struck a match and looked at the big octagonal clock on the wall. Nearly two. He composed himself and tried to sleep again. It was utterly impossible. He sat up and smoked a cigarette, then dressed with the intention of taking a walk.

A sullen, smothered boom shook the courthouse windows. Bob sat erect, listening, then hurriedly finished dressing, buckled his sixgun belt about him, and, grabbing his hat, ran from the office. As he came out on the sidewalk he saw a glimmer of light in the bank building.

He ran into the road where the dirt would silence the pound of his boots, and angled across the street toward the bank. The moon was just coming up, and as he drew near he could discern a group of horses held by one man. The fellow must have seen him at the same instant, for his gun blazed and Bob heard the whine of the slug as it cut the air above his head. He threw himself down behind the plank sidewalk and opened fire.

Men were streaming from the rear of the bank now, and the horses were milling about as each sought his mount and flung himself into the saddle. One of the animals broke away, running along the side of the bank toward the street. As its owner started after it, cursing in fear of being left afoot, Bob shot him. He stumbled on for a few yards then plunged forward on his face.

The others were mounted and reining away. One of them turned in Bob's direction and a ray of moonlight struck him. It was the short, red-headed man! In his eagerness Bob left the protection of the planks and started running toward him. The red-headed man flung a hurried shot at him, then wheeled his horse and spurred after his companions.

The hammer of Bob's Colt fell on an empty shell, and he hurriedly holstered the weapon. His horse was in the corral back of the courthouse, and precious minutes would be required to catch and saddle him. Bob glanced swiftly about. The horse of the dead outlaw had caught the reins in a crack in the sidewalk and was standing passively. He hurried to the animal, flipped the rein free and flung himself on his back. Kicking the animal into motion, he sped down the street on a course parallel with that taken by the outlaws.

When he finally passed the last straggling buildings, he caught sight of them. They rode in a compact group of four. Bob dug the spurs deep and sent the horse in swift pursuit.

Across the rangeland they sped, headed for the hills beyond the Kady. Bob reloaded his gun, wishing at the same time that he had a rifle. Gradually he gained on them; then one of the group swung off at a tangent. Presently another left the band and shot off to the right; then a third. Bob continued after the remaining man.

For an hour they rode as fast as their horses could travel, Bob slowly but surely closing the distance between them. He called to the other to halt and when he was not obeyed raised his gun to its highest angle of fire and flipped the hammer. He thought he saw the horse ahead of him falter, then surge forward with a renewed burst of speed.

The pound of solid ground beneath his horse's hoofs told Bob he was on the trail which led to the Tumbling T. Presently Tomlinson's buildings loomed up ahead of them, vague and shadowy in the faint moonlight. The bandit was heading directly for them, probably hoping to lose his pursuer in the gloom. The fellow cut between bunkhouse and corrals and for awhile was lost to view. Bob continued his course, passed the outbuildings, then rounded the corrals. Bandit and horse had disappeared.

Bob drew rein, glancing about him alertly. Back in the bunkhouse he could hear the Tumbling T punchers' excited voices as they sought the reason for the disturbance. Then he caught sight of movement close to the ground and some hundred feet ahead. He rode forward cautiously. It was the bandit's horse, down and evidently breathing his last.

Bob wheeled and headed for the ranch house, for a light had flared in the living room. He stopped at the hitching rack and, dropping to the ground, ran across the gallery. The door opened and he found himself gazing at June Tomlinson. She held a kimona about her and was carrying a lamp.

"Bob! What is it?"

"Bank holdup," he explained hurriedly. "I chased one of the outfit out here and shot his horse. The fellow's on foot somewhere."

"He's inside," she said. "I heard him open a window."

Bob raised his voice. "You Tumblin' T men! Surround the house!"

Shouts from the bunkhouse answered him, and men began streaming from the squat building. Bob stepped inside the room, gun in hand, and glanced about him.

Quite suddenly the dining-room door was thrown open, revealing a man in the entrance.

He was crouched, level gun extended before him. In the lamplight his face showed white and strained, the lips tight, the eyes burning. Bob stood staring at him, his gun pointed toward the floor.

"Dick!" cried the girl, stark agony in her voice.

"Yeah, it's me!" Dick's voice was harsh, grating. "You, Bob, get outa my way! You hear me? I won't be taken! Get outa my way!" His hand had tensed about the gun and a loud double click sounded as the hammer was drawn back.

"Don't! Dick—please!" cried June, and flung herself at him.

The paralysis which had gripped Bob left him. June was rushing toward this mad, cornered youth who was about to let the hammer slip from beneath his rigid thumb. June, the girl Bob loved more than life itself! He uttered a hoarse warning shout and bounded forward, intending to push her out of the line of fire.

And then, immediately before him, the gun spat red!

Bob never heard the sound of the explosion. A mighty weight struck him and he sank down—down—down into abysmal darkness.

CHAPTER IX

DICK'S PROMISE

IT was noon of the next day when Bob opened his eyes and gazed at the ceiling rafters in one of the Tumbling T ranch house bed rooms. He was aware of a certain stiffness which seemed centered in his neck, and found that the lower part of his head was bandaged. With an effort he lowered his eyes to find himself looking into the face of June Tomlinson. Her anxious gaze was fixed on him almost pleadingly, and she was holding his hand tightly between both her own.

"Miss—June," he said weakly. He found it an effort to speak.

"Bob! I'm glad you're awake. Don't move; you've been hurt."

His brain puzzled over this for a moment, and gradually the details of that calamitous meeting in the ranch house living room came back to him. At first the most vivid recollection was that flash of fire before his eyes. It was from a gun; a gun in the hands of—

June saw his face suddenly cloud. "Dick!"

"Yes. Oh, Bob, it was dreadful! Dick, your friend."

He gazed at her almost fiercely. "Did they get him?"

"No. He ran through the front doorway, jumped on the horse you left at the rack, and got away before the boys could saddle up."

"Do they know who it was?"

"No. I didn't tell them. I said I didn't know."

The strained look left his face. "Don't ever tell, June. He was cornered, desperate. He had to shoot his way out. It was my fault; I reckon he thought I was goin' to tackle him. Don't tell."

"I won't." The tears came to her eyes and she blinked and caught her lip between her teeth.

"Where am I hit?"

"Through the neck. You were unconscious last night and all this morning. It's just a little past noon. I'll give you some medicine the doctor left, and then you must sleep."

She raised his head and held the glass to his lips. Things were becoming hazy. Bob swallowed the stuff and dropped back on the pillows. His last waking memory was one of a fair face with deep violet eyes and an aura of golden hair in which the sunbeams danced.

When he awoke again she was gone, but he could hear voices in the next room. His brain was clear; he felt much stronger. And he was hungry.

The door opened noiselessly and June looked in at him. He grinned.

"If you'll fetch my clothes, ma'am, I'll be gettin' out of here."

She came in quickly then, her eyes wide with delight. "You'll do nothing of the sort," she told him severely. "Don't you realize that you are badly hurt? Why, it will be days before you can leave that bed."

The grin persisted. "Shucks! That slug didn't hit

anything vital; just stunned me, like they crease a wild horse at a water hole."

"Just the same you stay in bed until the doctor orders otherwise. Now take some more of this medicine."

A swarthy face appeared at the doorway. "Ees all right? He can spik weeth us?"

"Yes; you can come in, Joe."

The Mexican, followed by the towering Ace, tiptoed into the room. June administered the medicine and left them.

"Ees good to see you mak the smile," said Joe, his dark face beaming.

"Bet yore boots!" Ace echoed heartily. "Bob, I shore thought you'd drawed yore number. Who was it?"

"One of the five that robbed the bank. I heard them blow the safe and broke up the party. One of them rode into the moonlight and I recognized him as the red-headed jigger. How about that fella I winged?"

"They planted him this mornin'. Nobody seemed to know who he was." Ace jerked his head toward the door. "Frank Enright and Dutch Trumbauer are in the livin' room with Tomlinson. They want to see you. Reckon Frank is anxious to turn his boys loose."

"Don't let him do it until I'm up again," urged Bob. "He'll go in there all spraddled out and mess things up."

"You're right as rain." Ace craned his neck to look through the doorway. "Here they come now."

June entered with a bowl of broth, the two cattlemen behind her.

"I'm not sure that you should have so many visitors,"

she said, "but Mr. Enright and Mr. Trumbauer have come some distance to see you. I told them they could talk while you ate your broth." She assisted him to sit up in bed, propping pillows behind his shoulders. The two cattlemen shook his hand gravely.

"Glad to see you sittin' up, anyhow," said Enright.

Trumbauer beamed on him. "Py golly, it was a close shave, ain't it?"

"As close as I want. Did the robbers get anything?"

Enright answered. "No they didn't—thanks to you. They had a gunny sack filled, but the jigger that was totin' it dropped it just outside the bank. If you hadn't busted up the party there would 'a' been a lot of punchers without pay. Bob, I reckon it's about time I turned my wolf loose, ain't it?"

"Not yet, Frank. Wait until I'm up. I want you to realize that this cleanup will be something other than a mad dash into the hills. It's got to be planned, and every detail thought out in advance. And furthermore, we must not let a word of it get around until we're ready to spring the trap. Don't talk, not even to your own men."

Enright sighed resignedly. "Well, hurry up and get well then."

"Sure!" echoed Trumbauer. "And in the meanwhile, ve our guns vill be bolishing, not?"

His visitors finally left and June removed the pillows from behind him. Bob's eyes closed wearily. "I shore am a bother to you."

"You're no such thing!" June was still protesting when he fell asleep.

The sun had gone down when he awoke again, to

find little Doc Witherspoon in the room. From the kitchen came various savory aromas.

"Hello, Doc," said Bob. "When are you goin' to let me eat a real meal?"

The other eyed him keenly, took his temperature, felt his pulse.

"You have the constitution of a mule," the little doctor said almost complainingly. "I'll have to let you eat or you'll go on a rampage. Sit up now and I'll dress that wound."

"How long will I be laid up?"

"At the present rate of mend you'll be on your feet in two days. I know now why they use so many forty-fives out here. They have to put a hole as big as a rabbit burrow in you cowboys to keep you down."

June brought Bob his supper—quite a substantial one after the broth—and when he had finished eating he felt so strong that he cautiously sat up, dropped his feet to the floor, and attempted to stand. The effort was a failure, and he reluctantly sank back on the bed. He concluded that he had lost a lot of blood, but knew that rest and the proper food would soon remedy that.

June returned for the dishes, straightened his covers, and, bidding him good-night, extinguished the light and left the room. Bob lay there in the dark, thinking. Dick had put him here, but he felt no resentment. Friendship tested over a period of years is not so easily destroyed. This had been the act of a Dick temporarily irresponsible, a youth crazed with fear and remorse and the shame of having had his wrong-doing discovered by the girl he loved. Bob liked to think that even in such desperate straits Dick had not tried to kill him. It would have been simple at that short range to place a bullet between his eyes or in some other vital spot.

His thin blood burned hotly at thought of the men behind Dick's criminal act. He remembered the conversations between Markley and the suave Duke Haslam. Had Duke let the boy alone, he would now be riding on the side of the law instead of against it. Just as surely as Haslem controlled the trigger finger which had sent John Rutherford to eternity, did he direct the shot that had nearly made Dick a murderer. There in the darkness Bob swore again to stamp out forever Duke Haslam, Kurt Dodd, and the whole wicked gang they dominated.

A slight sound at one of the windows caught his attention. The sash had been raised, and through the opening came a sharp whisper. "Bob!"

"Who is it?" Unconsciously Bob lowered his own voice.

"Dick. I'm comin' in."

Bob heard the scrape of Dick's boots against the window casing, followed by soft footfalls. The next moment, Markley was kneeling beside the bed, a vague shape in the darkness. His eager hands found Bob's arm, gripped it with crushing, nervous intensity.

"Bob, old son! How you makin' it?"

"Fine, Dick." Bob's voice was light and he was grinning in the darkness. "You're a hell of a shot."

"Bob, I never meant to do it. I swear that hammer slipped from under my thumb! It was a new gun, and the spring was stiff. I slewed it off to one side, but when I saw you fall I thought shore I'd killed you."

"Nobody but you and June and I know," said Bob quietly. "I was unconscious and couldn't give you away, and June wouldn't."

He heard the young fellow utter a gasp of glad surprise. "Nobody knows it? She didn't tell?"

"No."

He could feel Dick trembling. Markley got to his feet and stood by the bed, taut in every muscle. "She shielded me! Even after—after—! Bob, do you know what that means?" His voice was vibrant with emotion.

"I reckon it means that she—cares for you." Bob winced as he said it, but in the darkness Dick could not see.

"It cain't mean anything else! Bob, I'm nearly crazy! Ever since I saw her that day I've loved her. And I doubted, Bob. Even though I played the game like I was shore of myself, I doubted. But she must love me. She must!"

Bob spoke almost fiercely. "Dick, you've got to quit this thing! Now! Before it's too late. For her sake you got to quit."

Dick stiffened. A crack of light had appeared at the bottom of the closed door. "Somebody's comin'," he said.

"Take it easy. Remember, nobody knows. You're in the clear, boy."

"That's right." Markley seated himself on the edge of the bed. Soft footfalls sounded in the hall.

"Who is it?" asked Bob.

The door opened and June Tomlinson, a lighted lamp in her hand, entered. Her gaze fell on Dick and for a moment she stood regarding him, eyes wide with surprise; then she softly closed the door.

"I had to come," Dick told her simply. "I wanted to tell Bob that it was an accident. He jumped toward me, and the hammer slipped from under my thumb. I've been waitin' outside ever since dark for a chance to slip in and tell him about it."

"I'm glad, Dick," she said quietly. "I felt that it must have been unintentional. I didn't see how it could be otherwise, after the years—"

"Yes, I know. I reckon you think I'm a skunk, June. But I'll make up for it! I swear I will!"

June placed the lamp on a table and seated herself by him on the edge of the bed. "Then you must begin at once, Dick. Quit this bunch you are running with. Become a deputy under Bob, or take a place on our spread. Both of us want to help you."

Dick's shoulders drooped and he stared moodily at the floor. "Sometimes a fella gets in so deep—"

"Never too deep to pull out, Dick." She placed an encouraging hand on his arm. "Especially with friends who want to help."

He slowly straightened and a look of determination came into his face.

"You're right. It's not too late." He got to his feet. "Take care of yoreself, Bob. June, look after him. I'm leavin'." He started toward the window, but June stopped him.

"You can go out the regular way, Dick. Father is in bed, and he doesn't know anyhow."

Dick followed her from the room. When she entered the living room she placed the lamp on the table and followed him to the gallery. There he turned and gripped her hand almost fiercely.

"June, I shore cain't tell you what I think of you for shieldin' me. But I'll never forget it; never!"

"Prove it to me, Dick."

He nodded somberly. "I will. Good-night, June girl."

Descending the steps, he circled the house to where he had left his horse. He was elated, lifted above himself, enthralled. June must love him, he told himself; unbelievable as it seemed, she must care for him. If he only had enough money! He dismissed the subject with a sharp frown and turned his horse toward Lariat. At the moment he felt very confident, entirely sure of himself.

It was late when he reached town, but lights still shone in the Paris. Dick dismounted outside the place and pushed through the swing doors. He saw Duke Haslam lounging at the end of the bar, a cigar between his thick lips. Dick went directly to him.

"Want to talk with you, Duke," he said shortly.

Haslam frowned. "This isn't the wisest thing to do," he complained. "Go into the office through the dining-room, and be sure nobody sees you."

Dick sauntered out and through the deserted lobby and dining-room. He stood in the dark office until Haslam arrived and lighted the lamp.

"Duke, I'm through."

Haslam straightened and eyed him coldly. "So?" he said. "Sit down."

"I don't want to sit down. I'm through. You heard me. It's no use tryin' to talk me out of it."

"So you don't want that ten thousand after all?"

"I want it bad enough, but I'm goin' to get along without it." Dick spoke fiercely. "Haslam, I shot Bob Lee last night; left him for dead. That he's livin' is no fault of mine. But he refused to tell who did it; he protected me, and so did Miss June."

"And for that reason you've decided to quit."

"Yes."

Haslam's face went hard. "You're crazy as hell! Through? You're just beginning! You took my money and you contracted to take more of it. Well, you're living up to your agreement."

"Yeah?" Dick's face went ugly too. "I'd like to see you make me."

"I intend to." Haslam eyed him scornfully. "I told you I'm running this show. You're taking orders, not giving them. Remember that pay-roll messenger of Rutherford's—old Charley Boggs, who was shot on the trail and robbed? Well, I hold your signed confession to that job."

Dick stared at him. "Are you loco?"

"No; just cautious. That receipt you signed—remember? The paper was folded so that you read only a part of it. The part you didn't read consists of your confession."

"Why damn yore soul, Haslam! I'll kill you for that!"

Duke's voice was contemptuous. "No you won't. That paper will come to light if anything happens to me. They'd string you higher than a kite. What chance would you have with June Tomlinson then?"

Dick glared at him. "You keep her name out of it!"

"Sure." Haslam quite suddenly changed. He laughed.

"Forget it, kid. Sit down; I want to talk with you. No use bucking against the snubbing post; you're thrown and hog-tied and may as well make the most of it. I got some plans that will earn you and me both some money. And that's the keynote of success, Dick— money. With it you can buy anything from a pair of socks to a woman's honor. Believe me, they don't say no when you wave a bundle of banknotes under their noses, or shake a poke of gold pieces at them!

"What chance do you stand with any girl as long as you are poor? Get the dough! Feather your nest while you're young and healthy, and live long to enjoy it afterwards! Come on; sit down. Try some of that whisky. It's a special brand guaranteed to brighten your outlook on life."

Dick, still scowling uncertainly, sat down. He drank, and he drank again. Haslam saw to it that the special brand which so improved one's outlook was not spared. And under the mellowing influence of the liquor and the persuasive, oily tongue of Duke Haslam, Dick's good resolutions melted away to nothingness, and when at last he walked unsteadily from the office, one arm was about Haslam's shoulders and he was more deeply involved than ever.

Chapter X

THE FIRST LINK

ONE week later, Bob and his three deputies rode from the Tumbling T and headed for the hills behind the Kady. Each carried a Winchester in the saddle boot and a blanket roll behind the cantle. Preparations for the big drive were under way.

They swung across the rangeland at a smart foxtrot, passing in time the north corner of the Tumbling T and that part of the Kady lying between them and their destination. Presently they entered the arroyo which served as an entrance to the hills, and pulled their mounts to a walk.

"Haven't seen Dick lately," said Ace suddenly. "Wonder where he's keepin' himself."

"Haven't seen Kurt Dodd either, or Bradshaw," said Deuce. "Funny how they never show up in town when things are quiet."

"They ees not need w'at you call the abblebi," offered Joe.

"Apple pie?"

"No, no! W'at you say w'en you are some place where you ain't?"

"Oh; you mean alibi!"

"Funny about Dick," persisted Ace. "He might have dropped in at the Tumblin' T to see how Bob was gettin' along." He slanted a sidelong glance at their leader. Ace remembered Bob's evasion when asked who had wounded him.

"He did stop in," Bob told them. "The night after I was shot. You and Joe had gone. Reckon I forgot to mention it. . . . Well, let's get down to business. When we reach the rock basin Ace and I found, we'll separate and each take a set of tracks and run them down. If you come across a park with stock in it, draw a map locatin' it, together with landmarks. Then find the way out of the hills from that park."

"Suppose we draw a blank?" asked Deuce.

"When you're sure it is a blank, return to the basin and take another set. There must be a dozen leadin' from that place. When they're all run down, go to Lariat and wait for the rest of us."

"Speakin' about not bein' in town," said Deuce, "I noticed that Pete Grubb has vamosed. If he's joined up with Dodd and we catch him, we might squeeze some information out of him. He's a weak sister."

Bob nodded his agreement, and they rode on. Presently they came to the little park where Bob and Ace had found the branding fire, scouted it, and continued their way to the rocky basin. Here they separated, each taking to one of the diverging gullies. Bob turned into the draw he had previously followed, remembering that the red-headed man and his companion had left the park where he had surprised them by a trail which as yet he had not explored.

He finally reached the place, to discover that the cattle had been moved. Further investigation showed the cabin to be deserted and the pole corral empty.

Here was ample grazing and a spring of good water, so Bob picketed his horse and ate a cold lunch. Finished, he produced paper and pencil and carefully mapped his progress to this point, then repacked and resaddled and continued his course.

He found the trail over which the red-head and his companion had left the park: a wide path now liberally marked with cattle sign. Bob soon discovered that the usual procedure of cutting out some of the bunch at each intersecting lateral had been followed, but refused to be diverted from the main trail. Even after all tracks had vanished, he stuck to his course, bringing up finally in a box canyon from which there was no outlet. He wasted the rest of the afternoon searching for a hidden exit, being forced in the end to camp for the night.

At daybreak he retraced his course to the last turning off point, and followed the dim tracks into an arroyo. After many turnings and twistings, each of which he marked on the map, he came, abruptly as was usual, to another park.

Like the first, this was bare of man or beast; but with ample evidence of recent occupation by both. Here, too, was a crudely built shack and a pole stock corral. A fresh cattle trail led through another draw. Bob judged that he was now in the very heart of the hills.

He had not gone very far when he received the distinct impression that he was being followed. Coming to a bend in the trail, he rounded it and pulled his horse to a stop behind a clump of bowlders. Nobody appeared, and at last he resumed his way.

The uneasy feeling persisted, however, and when at

last he heard the sharp report of a rifle somewhere behind him he instinctively ducked. There came a second shot, and then a third, but no accompanying whine of lead.

Bob returned to the bowlders where he had waited, and, dismounting, proceeded on foot to the bend in the trail. Peering cautiously from behind a rock he saw four horsemen approaching at a slow walk. Bob returned to his horse, mounted, and rode rapidly onward.

For some time past he had noticed the absence of lateral passages. The cattle trail extended in a broad, plainly marked, hoof-scarred path which no amount of ingenuity could conceal. The lack of branching ravines permitted Bob no opportunity to escape his pursuers by leaving the main trail. The sides of the gorge were too steep for a horse to negotiate, and all he could do was press onward in the hope of eventually striking an intersecting arroyo.

The path began a gradual descent, twisting with the convolutions of the hills and narrowing until cattle must have traveled through it no more than four abreast. A final turn and Bob involuntarily reined in.

Before him spread still another of these hidden parks, but many times larger than any of those he had previously encountered. Cattle by the hundreds browsed contentedly, and off to the right of the entrance was a long log cabin from the chimney of which smoke issued. Bob wheeled his horse intending to jump him back into the security of the passage he had just left.

He never reached his goal. A rope swished, and its noose circled his body, binding his arms to his sides. Desperately he strained against the hemp, managing to get his fingers on his gun, half drawing it from the holster. Then another rope settled over the first and he was almost jerked from the saddle as the slack was taken up.

"All right, Pete; git his gun," came the command, and when Bob turned his head to eye the speaker he recognized the short, stocky red-headed man with the dirty calfskin vest. He was standing atop a bowlder at one side of the entrance. Near him, holding an end of one of the ropes, was a long-faced melancholy appearing man. Glancing in the opposite direction, Bob saw two more. One was the stoop-shouldered ex-sheriff, Pete Grubb.

The latter shuffled forward a bit sheepishly at the red-head's command and jerked the sixgun from Bob's holster.

"Hello, Mouldy," said Bob coolly. "Looks like you got mixed up with bad company. Or have you belonged to this outfit right along?"

"Shut yore mouth, you!" ordered the red-head. "Go ahead, Pete; git that rifle too." Then, when his command had been obeyed, "Give him some slack. Pete, held that hawss of his'n."

He dropped from sight behind the bowlder, only to reappear mounted on a powerful bay horse. A rifle slanted across the saddle menacingly. "Take the ropes off'n him, and git yore animals. Lee, you'd better set powerful quiet. By cripes, I'm honin' to fill you with lead to pay you for them irons you put on me."

"Work yoreself into a rage," Bob suggested. "It'll help make you forget the rope necktie that you're goin' to wear as sure as I'm alive."

"You won't be alive long, fella. If it wasn't plumb against orders I'd drop you right now."

"Whose orders?"

"None of yore business! Shut yore trap. All right, you two; don't be all day gettin' them hawsses. One of you on each side, and if he makes a break plug him. By cripes, I hope he tries it!"

Pete Grubb walked ahead leading Bob's horse; the two rope throwers flanked him alertly, and the redhead brought up in the rear. Bob could almost feel the hot intensity of the red-lidded eyes that were focused on a spot between his shoulders.

Several men came from the cabin as they approached, to stand staring curiously at the captive sheriff. They were hard-faced men, of varied sizes and ages; but all wore guns, and all appeared quite ready to use them.

"This all you got, Shab?" asked one of them. Bob mentally noted the name—Shab. It seemed to fit.

"Enough, ain't it? It's the second time the danged fool come nosin' around the hills. It'll be his last too! Git off yore hawss, Lee."

Bob dropped to the ground. Shab poked his rifle in its scabbard, dismounted, and came shuffling over to him with that peculiar gait Bob had noticed. He stood before Lee and let his evil eyes roam over him slowly.

"I reckon you know what you're lettin' yoreself in for," Bob reminded him. "I'm the law, and I have three deputies that are hell-on-wheels when they get started. They'll shore make you hard to find."

Shab spat. "I don't scare worth a damn. A fat chance they got to trail you back here. We know you come in

alone. Four of the boys picked you up back there in
the park where you—where you—"

"Put the cuffs on you. Wrestled you down and put
'em on you, Red. Handled you just like a sack of oats,
didn't I?"

"Dang you!" blazed Shab, and struck him viciously
in the face.

Bob reeled from the blow, his head snapping back
and tearing open the half-healed wound. Swift as a
flash his right leg came up, straightened, and a powerful boot-clad foot caught Shab in the pit of the stomach.
As the red-head doubled in agony, Bob leaped forward
and his right fist came up in a blow that lifted Shab
from his feet and hurled him flat on the ground.

They were on him then, fully a half-dozen of them.
Bob flailed about with fist and foot, elbow and knee;
but they swarmed over him like bees on a honey comb,
kicking, striking, gouging. He could feel the warm
blood from his wound trickling down his shoulder and
soaking his shirt.

Pete Grubb, little eyes alight with anticipation,
danced about the milling knot of men, sixgun balanced
and ready. For an instant Bob's head showed above
those of his assailants. Pete brought the barrel of the
heavy Colt down on his skull, and Bob wilted like a
boiled rag.

When he recovered consciousness he was in complete darkness and bound hand and foot. His neck was
throbbing and his head felt as though it had been
mashed to a pulp. For some minutes he lay fighting
the pain and nausea; then he became aware of the
drone of voices, audible above the intolerable buzzing

in his ears. Slowly he worked to a sitting position, his back against a wall. He concluded that he was in a leanto built against the cabin. The walls were of logs and the door was closed, probably padlocked.

Now that he had shifted his position the voices came to him less clearly. He lay flat again, moved about until the words became distinguishable. A bit of the chinking between the logs had dropped from its place, leaving an opening about an inch wide and two or three inches long. Bob peered through it, but could see nothing, and judged that the hole was beneath a bunk. The voices were those of several men playing poker, and for a while the conversation was confined strictly to the game.

Presently Bob heard the thud of hoofs outside the cabin, then the door slammed and a voice said, "Hello, gang. How's chances of sittin' in?"

It was Dick Markley.

One of the players answered. "Shore. Pull up a box." For a moment there was silence while the cards were riffled, then: "Got a friend of yores in the leanto. Bob Lee."

"Bob Lee!"

"Yeah. Come traipsin' in here followin' cattle sign. Gloomy and Sam roped him while he was settin' his horse admirin' our layout."

"Did he put up a scrap?"

"I'll tell a man he did! The son-of-a-gun dang near busted my jaw. Holy bobcats, but he can fight! And Shab was fit to be tied. Lee rubbed it into Shab about wrasslin' him down and puttin' irons on him, and Shab hit him square on the jaw. Lee ups and kicks Shab in the belly and socked him so hard on the chin he come near to knockin' him into Cactus County. Shab took the count—five or six of 'em in fact. We jumped Lee, and Pete Grubb beaned him with a pistol bar'l. I reckon he's still asleep."

"What does Shab aim to do with him?"

"Well, he cain't do nothin' until we hear from the boss. But if Shab had his ruthers he'd likely stake him out on a ant hill for a day or two, then hang him in a tree, soak him with kerosene, and flip burnin' matches at him."

"For Pete's sake!" came an impatient voice. "Is this a poker game or a sewin' circle? Who can open this danged pot?"

"I'll open her," said somebody, and from then on the conversation reverted to poker.

The thin streak of light beneath the leanto door became dimmer, the surrounding objects less distinguishable. A man, evidently the cook, quit the game and started rattling pots and pans. Some time later, a number of horses circled the leanto, and from the sounds Bob judged that they were being stripped and turned into a corral. Presently the riders clumped by his prison and entered the cabin.

"Well, we hazed our bunch in," said one of them. "The last of 'em will get in tomorrow. Then we can drive as soon as we get the word."

"Where's Shab?" somebody asked.

"He's comin'. Say, that Texas fella musta busted him cock-eyed. His chin is blue and he shore is hard to get along with. . . . Hey, Doc, ain't that chow ready yet?"

"Comin' right up," answered the cook.

Another horse passed the leanto, and after awhile its rider entered the cabin. Bob was not left in doubt as to his identity. He had hardly stepped inside the room before his rough voice was berating the players.

"What in time do you hairpins mean by sittin' around like this? Ain't there nothin' to be done in this camp? Put up them cards and git this table outa the way. Dick, yore hawss is standin' outside. Turn him into the corral. Doc, dish up the grub."

"Comin', Shab. How about Lee; you goin' to feed him?"

Shab uttered a string of oaths. "If I catch you feedin' that lousy son I'll bust you wide open! Let him go hungry; he won't be needin' food when I git the word to go ahead with him."

Bob's lips tightened and he rolled away from the opening. Dick was passing the leanto on his way to the corral and Bob thought he had detected an inclination on Markley's part to loiter. Bob continued rolling until he brought up against the outer wall. Presently he heard Dick's returning footsteps, and kicked lightly against the logs. The footsteps halted, then came a cautious voice: "Bob!"

"Right here," answered Lee softly. "Against the wall."

"Bob, I cain't do a danged thing for you now. Shab would drill me if he even thought I was talkin' to you."

"There's a hole in the chinkin' about opposite where I am now and close to the floor," Bob told him. "Reckon it's under a bunk."

"Keno," whispered Dick, and moved on.

Time passed. To Bob's ears came the clink of knife and fork, the rattle of plate and tin cup. He judged that there were at least a dozen men in the cabin. At last the scrape of chair and box announced the conclusion of the meal. Some of the men went outside; others started another game.

"Where's the lantern?" came the harsh voice of the red-headed man.

"Hangin' behind the stove," the cook answered. "I'll get it for you."

Bob rolled away from the wall and lay staring at the darkness overhead. A crack of light appeared under the leanto door, somebody fumbled with the lock, then the door swung open and Shab Cannon came in. Holding the lantern high, he peered through the gloom, red-lidded eyes glinting.

"Awake, huh?" he grunted. "Well, pretty soon you're goin' to sleep for a long, long while. The jack is shore goin' to be missin' from that seven-up combination. By cripes, I'd like to plug you right here and watch you squirm!"

Bob eyed him contemptuously. "You're yellow enough to do it. Maybe you'd better wrap some more rope around me, though, before you start."

Shab leaped forward and kicked him in the ribs. "Shut yore trap! I ain't takin' no lip from you!"

Bob threw caution to the winds. Doubling up his bound legs, he pivoted on his back and lashed out at Shab. Only Cannon's quick backward leap prevented the wicked blow from landing. The red-head was furious.

"Why, you dam' wildcat!" he yelled, and leaped forward again. Bob rolled away to avoid the booted feet, and before Shab could catch up with him Dick Markley ran through the doorway and grabbed his arms.

"Cut that out, Shab! What kind of man do you call yoreself, actin' that-away?"

"You keep outa this!"

Dick tightened his grip. "Hush up and listen to me! You're wanted in the cabin. Somebody's comin'. You hear me?"

Shab growled a profane protest, but Dick remained steadfastly between him and Bob, and the red-head finally slouched from the leanto. Dick followed closely, and the door was slammed. In the hope that Markley had contrived to leave the lock unfastened, Bob got to his feet and hopped over to the door. His hope was in vain; the padlock had been properly replaced.

At the approach of hoofbeats, he hopped back to his place by the wall. Lying down on the ground he placed his ear to the crack. The door opened and voices were raised in greeting.

"Howdy, boys," greeted the newcomer.

Bob stiffened and pressed his ear closer to the opening. One of the connecting links had been found. The man who had spoken was Kurt Dodd.

Chapter XI

A DEBT IS SQUARED

THE confusion subsided when the men had gathered about the table. The first voice was that of Shab.

"Kurt, I'm glad you come over. Let's git this business of the prisoner outa the way. What's to be done with him?"

"Get rid of him."

"Ha! Now you said somethin'! I'll fix his clock. Forty feet of rope and a nice high limb."

"Not that way, Shab. We'd be makin' a hero out of him. Every man within fifty miles of Lariat would be in the hills after us. Remember, we got to get a thousand head of stock to Vandervort as soon as we can. Lee must go accidental-like. That lets us out, and at the same time fixes things jest like we want 'em. When a sheriff dies in office, you know, his successor is appointed by the governor."

"How you aimin' to git rid of him?"

"All sorts of accidents can happen to a man. He can get mixed up in a landslide, his hawss can throw him on some rocks, he can bog down in quicksand, get caught in a stampede or drown in a river."

"That quicksand idea is no good, Kurt. There wouldn't be anything left of him." Bob recognized Cole Bradshaw's voice.

"Why kill him at all?" asked Dick. "Make him sign a paper sayin' things are too hot for him and that he's resignin' his job. Then escort him out of the country and have another sheriff appointed."

"That's shore a bright idee," sneered Shab. "I got a pitcher of him stayin' away. Friend of yores, ain't he?"

"Not now. He'd run me in as quick as he would the rest of you."

"That won't do, Dick," said Kurt. "We gotta be shore he's out of it for good. That's settled; the only thing remainin' is to decide how to fix him."

"That cattle stampede idea sounds good to me," said Bradshaw. "After a coupla hundred steers get done walkin' over a fella nobody could tell if he died before or after the stampede."

"The Bottle Neck was made to order for that," said another. "We got to drive through there anyhow. Knock him out and plant him plumb in the middle, then haze 'em through at a run."

Shab broke in eagerly. "Yeah! And that means we can string him up first! I'd kinda set my mind on that."

"All right," agreed Dodd. "That's settled. First thing in the mornin'."

"Why cain't we hang him tonight?" complained Shab.

"No sense in it. We'd have to keep his body here and if somebody did drop in on us we'd have a hard time explainin' how we got a dead sheriff for comp'ny. First thing in the mornin'."

Bob lay close to the wall listening to the callous discussion. The prospect was far from bright. Even if

Dick wished to help him there was little he could do. Shab had the padlock key, and even were Dick able to get possession of it he would be given no opportunity to use it. He was known as a friend of the sheriff, and as such would be closely watched.

Inside the cabin the talk switched to other channels, and presently Dodd and Bradshaw departed. Shab Cannon gave a curt order.

"You fellas turn in early; we got work to do tomorrow. And I'll be up and around most of the night. I don't want to catch anybody walkin' in his sleep."

"You talkin' to me?" asked Dick sharply.

"I'm talkin' to all of you. I don't want nobody monkeyin' around that leanto." Shab left the cabin and Bob heard him shuffle past his prison.

"Well, I'm goin' to turn in." Dick's voice came from a point directly over Bob's peep hole. Lee heard him walk across the floor; then came the tinny clink of dipper on water pail.

Markley returned to the bunk and pulled off his boots, dropping them noisily to the floor. Bob heard him swear softly. One of the gang asked,

"What you lose, Dick?"

The reply came from so close to Bob's face that he stiffened expectantly.

"Dropped a dollar. Rolled under the bunk." A match flared and Bob had a fleeting view of Dick's questioning eyes. He hissed softly to attract Dick's attention and drew back from the opening. A black object was thrust through the inch-wide crack.

Bob wormed his way along the wall until his bound hands came in contact with the object. Carefully he drew it through the opening—a long, thin-bladed butcher knife which Dick had undoubtedly purloined while getting the drink of water.

Reversing the knife, Bob wedged the handle securely in the hole and began the tedious process of sawing through the ropes which bound his wrists. The blade was sharp and in time the strands parted. Fully ten minutes were required to restore the circulation and work some of the stiffness from his shoulder joints. After that it was an easy matter to free his feet.

Bob removed his spurs and put them in a pocket, then set about exploring the leanto. This also was constructed of logs, with a roof of poles and sod which he might eventually work through if he had something to stand on. But the place was barren of box or barrel; barren, in fact, of everything but himself. The door was of heavy planking. There was no window.

He considered making a noise to attract Shab, overpowering the fellow when he stepped through the doorway; but he dismissed the idea. As a last resort it might work, but any sound of a scuffle would be heard in the cabin and would bring men to Shab's assistance.

Bob went around the walls painstakingly, feeling for crevices which might be enlarged. That hope, too, he soon abandoned. No chance to whittle one's way through a wall constructed of twelve-inch logs. The floor was of dirt, but with Shab prowling about his effort to escape would be detected before the opening was sufficiently large. He finally turned to the door as the most vulnerable part of the leanto.

The fastening, he judged, was a hasp and staple one, and presently his groping fingers found the end of the screws which protruded through the boards. From the location of these, he mentally traced the outline of the hasp; then, with the point of the knife, went to work.

The progress he made was slow, for the boards were of oak and he was forced to work entirely with the point of the blade, which soon dulled. When the point was rendered useless Bob snapped an inch off the end of the blade, thus forming a new and sharper one to continue the cutting. The whole time he had to keep an ear open for the prowling Shab, ceasing work at his approach.

It must have been well after midnight when the blade point finally penetrated the board above the hasp. Bob stopped to rest for a minute, then doggedly went to work on the bottom cut. His knife had been broken off so often that but a stub of the original twelve-inch blade remained, and he was forced to use the broken pieces, thus redoubling the labor.

The hours passed, and Bob, realizing that dawn must be only minutes away, worked feverishly. He was working with the last inch of blade, and that was dishearteningly dull. At last he felt the point slip through the wood. And at the same moment Shab Cannon's voice sounded at the cabin door.

"Come on, you dudes, roll out! Doc, git that breakfast goin'." Bob heard his heavy tread approaching the leanto. "Wake up, Lee. It won't be long now. You hear me?"

Bob retreated softly to the far end of the shack. "I hear you."

Shab returned to the cabin and entered it. Bob could hear his raucous voice berating the tardy risers.

It was now or never. Bob put his shoulder against the door and pressed steadily, firmly. There came a low splintering sound and the door flew open. In an instant he was outside. Closing the door and hastily fitting the v-shaped piece holding the hasp into place, Bob ducked around the corner and ran silently toward the pole corral. It was still dark, only the gray in the east suggesting the dawn that was so near.

He found his saddle and bridle on a rail where somebody had tossed them, and from the former took down the rope tied to the horn. The blanket roll had been removed. Climbing into the corral he set about cutting out his horse. It seemed that everything went haywire. It was dark and the horses were skittish; they milled about in a most disconcerting manner, and Bob finally gave up trying to catch his own mount, concentrating on the animal nearest him. The noose finally settled over the neck of a stocky bay.

A sudden hoarse shout cut the stillness, then came the profane voice of Shab Cannon calling his men. Bob dragged the horse to the side of the corral and threw a half-hitch around a post. Hastily he snatched the bridle from the rail and slipped it on the animal's head. It was too loose, but there was no time for adjustment. Seizing the saddle, he flung it on the horse, caught the end of the cinch and slipped the latigo through the ring. A hasty tug and it was tight.

Back at the cabin men were shouting, and Shab's voice was raised in vile imprecations. Bob reached the corral gate and swung it open in time to see the whole bunch running in his direction. One of them was far in the lead.

The fellow in advance flung a shot which surprised Bob by going wide. He was so close that Lee knew he could never swing his horse and gain the saddle in time to avoid him. He turned savagely and stepped toward the fellow. As he leaped at Bob, Lee recognized Dick Markley.

"Knock me out, for God's sake!" Dick panted.

Bob dropped the reins and swung. Dick seemed to fling himself at the moving fist; the blow landed on his chin and he went down. His hand, holding a revolver by the barrel, was extended toward Bob as he fell.

Lee seized it and flung two shots at the approaching bandits; then ran after his horse, which was moving at a slow jog along the corral fence, head held high to avoid stepping on the reins. Bob vaulted completely over the animal's rump and, bending low, seized the reins and kicked the horse into a wild run.

Lead cut the air about him and Shab's curses burned the air behind him; but the former missed the rapidly moving horseman, and the latter served only to speed his efforts. Bob swept around the corral, found a trail leading from the basin, and gave the horse its head.

Chapter XII

THE BIG DRIVE

B OB did not know where he was going, this trail being a new one to him. Provided it did not end in a box canyon, he did not care. The most important thing at the moment was to put a lot of distance between himself and the raging Shab.

As the light strengthened, he saw that he was following a well-marked gradually descending road. Presently he entered a gorge, which after a short distance debouched on a wide, hilly plain. Bob remembered the reference to the Bottle Neck and concluded that he had just passed through it. Before him was open country, and he knew he had crossed the mountain range to the valley beyond that in which Lariat was situated. Swinging to the south he rode along the base of the hills, coming in time to a road which cut through a pass above Kurt Dodd's spread.

Late that afternoon he reached the Tumbling T. June rode out to meet him, and he told his story while his tired horse stumbled the rest of the distance to the house. "I'll borrow a fresh horse and ride to Lariat after the boys," he finished.

"You'll do nothing of the sort," she contradicted firmly. "I'll send for them. You're in bad shape, Bob, between that wound and riding all day in the sun without a hat."

"I wish you'd send for Enright and Trumbauer too. Tell them to bring every hand they can spare. June, we've got those rustlers as shore as I'm a foot high! Got 'em penned up in the hills with their rustled stock."

"Unless your escape causes them to scatter."

"I think they'll bluff it out. They have a lot of cattle to drive, and if they leave them now they'll lose every head. But we must hurry."

An hour later, fed, bathed, and wounds attended to, Bob closed his eyes for a short nap. It seemed to him that he had been sleeping only a moment when June awakened him, but he felt refreshed, ready and eager for the task ahead of him.

His deputies had arrived and it was necessary that he relate for their benefit the adventures which had befallen him. He kept silent about the part Dick had played, giving them to understand that he had worked free of the ropes and had broken the lock on the door.

Dutch Trumbauer arrived with seven men, and Enright, with eleven more, appeared almost on his heels. Leaving their crews to find places on the veranda or down at the bunkhouse, the two bosses went into the living room where June, Tomlinson, and Bob and his deputies were gathered. Four rough maps were spread on the table before them.

Briefly Bob acquainted Trumbauer and Enright with the details of their search. "The boys report that in every case the trails they followed finally led to the basin where I was held. It is a central gatherin' place. From there they drive through a canyon and a long

park that narrows into what they call the Bottle Neck.
Last night this time there was one more bunch to come
in before the drive started. I figure that they got under
way some time this afternoon. It's bad country and
they won't move fast. They'd have to bed down their
stock over night in some park, finishin' the drive tomorrow.

"Now this is what we'll do: Enright, you and yore
eleven must hit the trail right now, crossin' the moun-
tains through the pass above the Kady. Cut to the left
and follow the hills to the Bottle Neck. It's marked on
this map so you cain't miss it. Post yore men on both
sides of the Bottle Neck and hold them there.

"The rest of us will ride to the flat where the trails
begin. In the mornin' we'll divide into four parties. I'll
lead one, and Ace, Deuce, and Joe will lead the others.
We'll move by four different routes to the central
gatherin' place.

"If the cattle are still in the basin, we'll wait until
they start the drive and follow them. If the cattle are
gone, we'll meet at the cabin and go after them. We'll
trail that herd and jump them at the Bottle Neck.
Run 'em through and into the hands of Enright's men.
That clear?"

"Clear as can be," said Enright. "Give me that map."

"Remember to keep yore men hidden until they
come through the Neck," Bob cautioned him. "There
may be as many as twenty of them, but you will have
the advantage of position and surprise. I want them
captured if possible."

Enright got up, placed the map in his pocket, and
went out to assemble his men. Presently they heard

the whole Big 4 crew swing past the house at a fast lope.

"Might as well start," Bob told the others. "We can travel together as far as that rock flat. Trumbauer, get yore men. Mr. Tomlinson, I'm sorry you cain't get in on this. Reckon you'll have to trust yore crew to me."

"No one else I'd rather trust 'em to," said Tomlinson. "June, tell the boys to saddle up."

As Bob and his friends were leaving the house they met June coming in. She grasped Bob by an arm and detained him until they were alone. For a moment they looked steadily into each other's eyes.

"What about Dick?" she asked softly.

"He goes free if I have anything to do with it. Dick's been dragged into this thing. When he promised to go straight, he meant it."

"I like to think so," she said. "Bob, take care of yourself."

She stood on the gallery watching as the excited men gathered in a compact body. Bob led them from the yard, flinging an arm upward in a farewell salute to her as he rode by. She answered mechanically, and when the gloom had swallowed them, sighed and turned back to the house.

Bob's party of eighteen rode across the Tumbling T and the Kady and into the arroyo which led to the rocky flat, holding to a swift pace until the rough going forced them to a walk. It was after midnight when they finally halted in the park where Ace had found the branding fire. At Bob's command they dismounted and pulled off their saddles, hobbling or picketing the horses in order that they would not stray. No fire was lighted, the men throwing themselves on the ground to talk and smoke and cat-nap.

"Frank should be through the pass by now," observed Deuce. "I sort of wish I was with him. Think of the fun he's goin' to have when that outfit comes stringin' through the Bottle Neck."

"There ees many w'at you call slip between the tin-cup and the mouth," Joe warned them. "May be they ron wrong way; then we have the fon, no?"

"Yeah. Two yeahs and a fond hope," said Deuce fervently. "I'd shore admire to line my sights on that red-headed gent Bob's been tellin' about. I'd fix him so he wouldn't hold water worth shucks."

"Py golly, shust give me at him von shot mit Gretchen here, und I scatter him the landscape over," swore Trumbauer. "Gretchen" was a sawed-off ten-gauge shotgun loaded with buckshot.

Deuce voiced a warning. "Fellas, you wanta be shore to keep well behind Dutch. It's the only place you'll be safe."

"With the charge he's got in that thing," said one of Trumbauer's men, "I'd as lief be in front of him as behind him. Some day the breech is gonna blow out and he'll scatter hisself the landscape over."

"If Dutch only knowed the way in, we could 'a' all gone with Frank. That load spreads from one side of the valley to the other; Dutch could drive horses, cattle and rustlers into the Bottle Neck without any help."

"Maybe I do it yet," countered Trumbauer, unperturbed. "Ven der lead pegins to fly maybe you young squirts find pusiness somevere at the rear yet."

Dawn brought a cold breakfast and preparations to move. Almost before the sun's rays had touched the tops of the eastern hills they were on their way. By mid-morning they had reached the rocky basin, and here again a halt was called while Bob divided them into four parties.

He led his own group into the arroyo he had followed before, Trumbauer at his side, two lean Texans from Tomlinson's spread bringing up in the rear. They met no one to challenge their passage, and at noon halted briefly in a park which Bob had previously explored. As before, he found it barren of men and cattle. A short rest and they pressed onward.

Near the entrance to the big central park they halted momentarily while Bob scouted ahead. As he had expected, the rustled stock had been driven from the basin. Signaling his men, they rode into the park, spreading out and advancing toward the cabin. A rifle spat viciously and one of the Texans clapped his hand to an arm and swore.

"Just nicked me," he explained quickly, grinning sheepishly. "I'm more scairt than I am hurt. Let's get that son-of-a-biscuit."

They broke their horses into a run, heading directly for the cabin. Bob saw a man duck from the door and race for the corral behind the leanto. While the other three continued toward the cabin, Bob pulled away so as to cut into the trail which led from the corral to the Bottle Neck, determined that the man who had been left as a precaution against pursuit would never have an opportunity to warn his companions on the drive.

He caught the flash of a running horse behind a clump of trees, and swerved so as to intersect the trail where it entered the gorge. The other rider reached the point before Bob. He was riding low, stretched along the neck of his lunging horse, and Bob had the merest glimpse of him as he thundered into the narrow passage.

Bob flashed in pursuit, calling upon his horse for everything it had. He closed the distance between them rapidly, although the other held his bent-over position, urging his mount forward with every bit of riding skill he possessed. Presently horse and rider flashed around a jutting clump of rock and were lost to sight.

Bob reached the bend, turned, then reined his horse so hard that the animal crouched on his hocks, sliding. The other had pulled up behind the bowlders and Bob caught the glint of sunlight on rifle barrel even as he recognized Dick Markley.

He acted instinctively, hurling himself from the saddle straight at the threatening weapon. Bob's extended hands found the rifle barrel, and as he landed on his feet he heaved, jerking Dick sidewise from the saddle. The weapon was torn from Markley's hands and tossed to one side of the trail. Then they were locked in each other's arms.

In Bob's powerful grip, Dick was helpless. Snatching the sixgun from Markley's holster, Bob pushed the other backwards and released him. For several seconds they stood looking at each other, panting from their exertions.

"There is no time to be lost," said Bob at last. "Get on yore horse and head up that lateral."

Dick gulped. "You're lettin' me go?"

"Yes. But take my warnin', Dick. Get out of this bunch and stay out. We're on their heels, and they're done! Get up that arroyo as quick as you can. And don't try to warn Kurt and Shab. Keep away from the Bottle Neck or I won't be able to help you."

He handed Dick's sixgun to him and motioned toward the rifle. "Better hurry; if my boys find you here it will go hard with you."

Dick stared at him for another moment, then walked over and recovered the rifle. Swinging into the saddle, he looked down at his friend.

"Bob," he said huskily, "you—you're white!"

Some of the bitterness within Bob welled forth. "Dick, cain't you see what this is costin' me? I'm a traitor to my badge—to the oath I took! This is yore last chance. If you cain't quit on my account, for God's sake think of June."

To them came the sound of iron-shod hoofs on rock. Dick wheeled his horse and rode rapidly into the arroyo. Bob mounted and spurred back to meet his companions. They drew rein, eyeing him questioningly.

"Rode up one of these side gullies," Bob explained tersely. "No time to hunt him. I'll stay here to be sure he doesn't ride back into this ravine. You boys go back to the cabin and bring the rest of them as soon as they arrive."

The three turned and jogged back toward the park, Dutch Trumbauer bobbing ludicrously in his saddle. Despite his years on the range Dutch had never acquired the easy seat of the born Westerner.

An hour later the entire seventeen swung around the bend, Ace, Deuce and Joe in the lead. Bob joined them without halting their progress.

"Meet anybody comin' in?"

"Nary a soul," Deuce answered. "Reckon they're all busy today. Heard yore man got away from you. You oughta got Dutch to shoot that blunderbuss up the lateral. Those danged buckshot travel in loops and spirals and can turn corners. Betcha he'd 'a' got the jigger!"

The afternoon was half gone when the gorge widened out into a long, flat park. Ahead of them the dust hung heavy in the air.

"That's the herd!" cried Bob jubilantly. "And ahead there where the valley narrows is the Bottle Neck. They must be near it now. Boys, spread out the width of the park. The dust will hide you from them. Close in at a lope. When you sight the drag, cut loose. Drive 'em through the gap into Enright's trap. Get goin'!"

With shrill yips of excitement the cowboys scattered. Eager fingers found sixguns and loosened them in their holsters; rifles were drawn from saddle boots and held ready across the pommels. At a smart lope the whole line moved forward.

The dust cloud thickened, and soon they could smell the animal sweat of many moving steers. They passed a laggard or two that had escaped the vigilance of the drag, and even above the noise made by their own horses came the tramp of many feet, the sound of plaintive bawling, the clash of horns.

Off to Bob's right Trumbauer's shotgun bellowed, and Bob caught a glimpse through the haze of an astonished drag rider. He raised his rifle and fired. More reports sounded along the line of advancing men.

Orange flashes stabbed the dust as answering shots were flung at them; the angry whine of lead was in the air. Bob could hear his men yipping wildly as they advanced. He tried to check them, fearful that in the haze the rustlers would break through their thin line.

They were almost in the Bottle Neck now, and the fire ahead of them had doubled in its intensity. Evidently the rustlers had thrown more men in the drag to protect their rear. Bob noticed that the flashes were drawing away from the center as though the opponents were attempting to reach the sides of the valley.

And then from the head of the herd came a crashing volley that echoed the length of the park. It puzzled Bob, and he checked his horse to listen. To his ears came the sudden appalling thud of hundreds of hoofs; through the thick dust between him and the Neck he caught a glimpse of wild eyes and tossing horns. The explanation of the shots came to him with a sharp chill of foreboding.

The wily Kurt Dodd had turned the big herd against his pursuers! The very cattle Bob sought to save was to be made the instrument of his destruction!

He glanced quickly to the right and then to the left, even as he wheeled his horse and sent him off at a frightened run. On either side of him men were bending over their horses' necks, angling at full speed for the sides of the valley. No such course was open to Bob; he was squarely in the middle of the park, and long before he could reach a place of safety his panicky horse must go down beneath the pounding, grinding hoofs of the stampeded cattle.

He rode straight ahead. No need for quirt or spurs; the animal beneath him was racing onward in long, terrified leaps. Bob himself felt the stab of a mighty fear. The cattle were gaining; every time he looked over his shoulder it was to find the glaring eyes and distended nostrils nearer. He conquered his momentary panic. If he were to save himself he would need all his courage, every bit of cool wit he could summon.

Slightly to the left and ahead of him, he caught sight of a low outcropping of rock. It was pitifully small, less than a few square yards in area and rising not more than a foot above the plain, but it must serve. He had the greatest difficulty in swinging his horse even the few degrees necessary. The animal seemed to know that its only hope of escape lay in holding to a straight course.

As they approached the spot, he kicked free of the stirrups, and, holding to the horn, swung out of the saddle. His feet touched the ground, were snatched from beneath him by the force of contact. He started moving his legs in a running motion, again lowered his body, matching the speed of his stride with that of the horse. Twenty feet from the rock cluster he released his hold, and was hurled over the surface of the ground, his momentum finally throwing him and sending him ploughing through the dirt. Desperately he scrambled to the protection of the rocks, flattening himself on the ground behind the low ridge.

A swift shadow crossed between him and the sun—another—a third. Steers jumping the rock! One of them stumbled, sprawled across Bob's body, legs thrashing wildly. The rock supported most of the steer's weight, but Bob felt thud after thud on the body above, a body that in a very short while had become a lifeless carcass, a mass of bloody flesh and bone.

Then the stampede had rumbled past, and he managed to crawl from beneath the litter which covered him. A heavy pall of dust hid the Bottle Neck from his sight. He started at a run toward the narrow passage. A horseman loomed up before him, and a shotgun roared almost in his face. Bob stopped abruptly, astonished to discover that he had not been blown to bits.

"Trumbauer! For gosh sake what are you tryin' to do!"

"Pob! Iss is you? Ain't you dead yet?"

"It's not yore fault that I'm not! Be more careful where you point that thing. Get down and let me have yore horse."

Dutch got awkwardly from the saddle. "Py golly! I must der buckshot out of der shell left, not?"

Bob flung himself into the saddle and rode swiftly toward the Neck. Half way there he ran into a body of horsemen who had just come from that direction. He peered through the haze, then shouted at their leader.

"Enright! What are you doin' in here?"

"Bob, what in time is goin' on? By Judas, we waited but nobody come through. Then we heard the heavy firin' and figgered somethin' had gone wrong. Where are the rustlers?"

Bob swore bitterly. "I told you to stick to yore post! Now you've left the Neck unguarded and every man of them has slipped through. Damn it, Frank! you've ruined the whole plan."

He spurred angrily past the crestfallen man and continued toward the gap. Deuce rode out of the dust and joined him. He was dirty and sweaty and boiling mad.

"Did you see Frank Enright? Dang him, he left the pass unguarded! We had 'em in a sack and he ripped the bottom plumb out!"

"You seen any of the rustlers?" Bob called to him.

"Nary a one. They pulled out of the way so that stampede could go by, then I reckon they saw Frank's men come through the pass and ducked out after the way was clear."

They rode swiftly, passing presently through the pall of dust into the clear air of the pass. Far out on the floor of the valley beyond rode a scattered band of horsemen that they knew were the rustlers. Closer in were two others, both riding as fast as their horses could travel.

"Ride that one down!" shouted Bob. "I'll take the other." He set out in pursuit of the horseman nearest him. The fellow rode on, crouched over his horse's neck, but the animal limped, and Bob gained rapidly. Presently he recognized the heavy form of Kurt Dodd.

When he had drawn close enough he opened up with his sixgun, and at the third shot Dodd's horse went down. The rider was flung hard, but was on his feet almost instantly, gun in hand. Evidently he had lost his rifle.

Lee flung himself from the saddle directly at the man. Even as Kurt's gun blazed, the barrel of Bob's weapon struck him on the wrist, causing his shot to go wild; then he had closed with the man, wrestling him over the uneven ground with the strength of a wild, unreasoning anger.

Kurt was by far more powerful and heavily built than Bob, but at this moment he was no match for Lee. Flinging Kurt from him, Bob drove a straight right into the fellow's face, and Kurt went down on his back. Before he could recover his dazed faculties, Bob had snapped a pair of handcuffs on his wrists.

Kurt sat up and swore sulphurously. "What the hell do you mean by this?"

"You'll find out soon enough," snapped Bob. "Yore horse is dead; start walkin'."

On the way back they were joined by Deuce, who also drove a captive before him. "Ain't I got the dangest luck?" bemoaned the deputy. "Out of the whole shootin' match I hadda go and get my loop on Mouldy Grubb! I'm plumb ashamed of myself."

The rest of the posse came surging from the Neck, but halted at Bob's signal. "It's no use," he told them grimly. "They're scattered all over. These two are all we get for our pains."

A humbled Frank Enright spoke. "It's all my fault too."

Bob shrugged. "What's done is done. You and Trumbauer and the boys stay here and gather the cattle. Ace, you and Joe come with us. We'll take the prisoners to Lariat and give Judge Bleek and Thad Poole somethin' to do."

CHAPTER XIII

THE TRIAL

THE trial of Kurt Dodd and Pete Grubb was set for a week later, justice in the cow-town of that day moving swiftly. Bail had been set at one thousand dollars, but for some reason was not furnished, and the two went to jail.

"Shore I could raise the money," Dodd told Bob. "But what's the use? By thunder, you arrested me, now you can feed me; and when the jury turns me loose, I'm gonna make you hard to find in this part of the country."

"You shore have my permission to try. I laid in that leanto and heard you plan my murder. I aim to show you up as the low-down rustler and killer you are."

Kurt's eyes gleamed malevolently. "I'll do my crowin' *after* the trial."

Bob placed the two men in different cells and dropped into prosecuting attorney Poole's office. "Hello, Thad. Reckon we'd better shape up the case against Dodd and Grubb."

"Sheriff, if you have no more evidence than you produced at the preliminary hearing, the men will go free."

"They won't if you put it before the jury in the right

way. These men were caught with a bunch of stolen cattle. Both of them were runnin' from my posse. Pete Grubb was with the gang that caught and disarmed me, and Dodd was the one who told them to do away with me."

"That's what *you* say."

Bob stiffened. "Meanin' what?"

"Don't misunderstand me. Personally I do not doubt that these men are guilty, but you must remember that in a court of law your unsubstantiated word is no better than that of Dodd or Grubb. The burden of proof, sheriff, is on us. They are innocent until we have proven them guilty."

"The stolen cows were driven across the Kady, and a holdin' corral and brandin' fire were found on Dodd's property."

"You mean somebody drove cattle across Dodd's spread and, presumably, did some branding. Can you prove the tracks were made by stolen cattle? or that the fire you found had been used for branding? Can you prove that the corral held stolen stock at any time? I say that you can not. The park in which you found the stolen stock is not on Dodd's spread, and you can be sure that whoever defends him will make this clear."

"But dang it, man! Kurt was ridin' with those rustlers."

"Where is your proof? You jumped a bunch of rustlers driving cattle toward what you call the Bottle Neck. In the fight which followed—a fight in so much dust that it was impossible to recognize any of your opponents—the rustlers escaped and scattered. In the pursuit you shot Dodd's horse and arrested him, while one of your deputies caught and disarmed Pete Grubb. What does that signify? I can tell you right now what their defense will be. They, too, were on the trail of the rustlers. They, too, had followed the drive hoping to discover where the cattle were being taken. When the rustlers broke through the Neck, they followed. Instead of fighting against you, they were fighting with you."

Bob eyed him grimly. "I see I cain't count on any help from you in cleanin' up this county. All right; I'll do it alone." He stamped angrily from the room.

Afterwards, as he sat in his little office thinking things over, he decided that he should be grateful to Thaddeus Poole for thus clearly demonstrating the difficulty of proving his case. He realized that he had been taking things too much for granted. Knowing Kurt Dodd to be guilty, he had assumed that his straightforward story would convince any jury that the charge against Dodd and Grubb was based on actual facts and not on theory. It seemed now that he was assuming too much; that somebody else must support his story in order to make it stick.

He got up and went out to the jail. "Get Pete Grubb for me," he instructed the jailer.

Pete came shuffling from his cell, weak chin sagging in wonder. "Whadda you want, Lee?"

Bob took him by the arm and marched him into the office, then closed the door and bolted it. "Sit down," he said.

"Now," he went on, "me and you are goin' to have a little talk. I just came from the prosecutin' attorney's office, and he outlined yore defense for me. It seems that you ain't a rustler, Pete, but a God-fearin' man who was helpin' his employer recover stolen stock. Yes, sir. When Deuce caught you, you were chasin' those rustlers with murder in yore heart. You was just foggin' yore horse to beat the band in an effort to catch up with one of them and wipe out his miserable life. And Thad tells me that the jury is goin' to believe you. They're goin' to set there and weep because you've been misunderstood by a pore dumb sheriff like me."

"Why—why—I don't know what you're talkin' about!"

"That's all right, so long as you understand this: Me, I know that you socked me over the head with a sixgun while I was fightin' six real men. I know you were with the bunch that roped me and condemned me to be tromped all out of shape by a bunch of frightened steers. I know you're a lyin', thievin', cowardly little runt. The jury might let you off, but I never will. After what you did it's a personal issue between us. I'm servin' notice on you that if you're acquitted, I'll hand you a gun right there in the courtroom, slap yore face, and dare you to try to use it! And if that don't make you fight I'll kick yore pants out of the room and camp on yore trail and pester you until you do fight. And when you finally go for that gun, I'll kill you deader than Julius Caesar!"

Grubb's face was a pasty white. "Now, Lee, you ain't got no call to talk thataway!" he protested shakingly. "You ain't allowed—"

"Don't tell me what I'm allowed to do! I'll do as I please, you lousy little thief! I'm out to get yore whole dirty crowd, and the sooner you realize it the better off you'll be."

"I don't know why—"

"You don't know anything; but get this in yore head. If you go free you might as well make yore will; unless—" He broke off, watching the furtive little eyes brighten with hope.

"Yeah?"

"You come clean at the trial, Pete, and I'll go just as far in the other direction to protect you. Nobody will hurt you. Just give us the whole story, tellin' where Shab and Kurt are hooked up, and where Kurt and Haslam are connected—"

"Haslam!"

"Haslam. Duke Haslam. He owns the Paris, Pete. I know as well as you do that he's behind the whole thing. So, as I said, you just speak right up and I'll guarantee that nobody will hurt you, for the simple reason that I'll put everybody that would want to hurt you where they won't have a chance even to cuss you to yore face. And if you don't help me—well, you'll be sleepin' peacefully with a couple cubic yards of dirt for a blanket. What do you think?"

Pete sat there staring at him, stark terror in his eyes. Gradually the fear disappeared; perhaps he was thinking of the powerful friends behind him. At last he got up angrily. "Whadda you mean by talkin' thataway to me?" he blustered. "Tryin' to corrupt me—"

"Shut up! What do you want to do—sit, stand, or lie down?"

"W-whadda you mean?"

"I mean you're not goin' back to the cell where you

can tell all our secrets to yore honest, persecuted boss. Much as I dislike lowerin' myself, you're goin' to live with me until the trial. When I'm here in the office, you'll be with me, chained to a chair or a cot; and when I go out, you go along. It's goin' to be tough, but it's got to be done. And the whole time I'll be remindin' you of my offer."

"I'll set," said Grubb gloomily. "But this ain't reg'lar at all. I never treated a prisoner of mine like this."

"You never took enough prisoners to learn how to treat 'em," said Bob, and proceeded to handcuff him to a chair.

In the days which followed Bob was as good as his word. Everywhere he went he took Pete Grubb. They walked together, ate together, slept in the same room. And at least once each day Bob quizzed him. Who hired the man to kill Rutherford? Who bought the stolen cattle? What part did Haslam have in the scheme of things? And when Pete refused to answer, he would take down his sixgun and oil it while Grubb looked on with sagging jaw and staring eyes.

It was the day before the trial that Pete finally broke.

"Why don't they do somethin'?" he suddenly wailed. "Why don't they git me a lawyer? I'm entitled to one, ain't I?"

"Who do you mean by 'they'?" asked Bob quickly.

"The gang! Shab, Bradshaw, Dick."

"And Haslam?" prompted Bob.

"Yes, by Godfrey! Him too! I've done his dirty work without kickin', and now he leaves me in the lurch! I'll tell everything! I will, so help me Hanner!"

"Pete, I'll call a witness and we'll put it in writin'."

"No! No, I cain't do that! If they knowed they'd kill me before I got a chance to talk. I tell you they'd shoot me right down while we was walkin' along the street together! I'll tell it on the witness stand. But you got to protect me, Lee; you gotta!"

"I'll have the bracelets on 'em before you get their names out of yore mouth. Now you rest easy. Better let me write it out for you."

"No." Pete shook his head stubbornly, face ashen. "No. I'll tell it from the stand. You got to wait."

With this Bob was forced to be content. Pete was adamant in his refusal. He feared Bob because he knew Lee would carry out his threat to the full; but he feared Duke Haslam even more.

Night brought almost as big a crowd to Lariat as had election eve. Cattlemen streamed in from outlying districts, anxious to be present when the first aggressive step of the Cleanup Party was taken. Cole Bradshaw rode in with Dick and the whole Kady crew. Bob, watching from the office window, pointed them out to Pete Grubb.

"There they go, Pete, probably most of them members of the gang that escaped through the Bottle Neck. They're safe because we have no legal proof against them. Me and you, Pete, will see to it that they don't ride out of town so gaily as they rode in."

Ace, Deuce, and the Mexican arrived that evening. They had been carrying on the range and stage-line patrols, and Bob had seen them only occasionally during the week. They made a brief report and departed to maintain order in town. The lights blazed in saloon and gambling hall later than was usual, and men were still discussing the coming trial when Bob and his prisoner turned in.

They arose early in order to avoid the crowd at the breakfast table. Pete was tight-faced and gloomy; he barely touched his food, and seemed relieved to get back in the office. Bob unshackled him and allowed him the freedom of the room.

"Take it easy, Pete. Nothin's goin' to happen to you."

Pete mopped his damp forehead. "I ain't got the chance of a hydrophoby dawg. If I don't talk, you're gonna kill me; if I do, Duke Haslam will see to it if he gits half a chance."

A knock sounded, and Bob opened the door to find the prosecuting attorney and a stranger standing in the corridor.

"This is Sylvester Fish," introduced Poole. "Honorable 'torney for the defense." Poole was steady enough on his feet, but his face was a deeper shade of purple than was usual and his nose shone like a beacon.

"Come in," Bob invited shortly.

Fish was a small skinny man with the sharp features of a buzzard. The way his outthrust head bobbed at the end of his thin neck emphasized the likeness. He nodded jerkily.

"This my client? Like to speak with him. Mind stepping outside?"

Bob moved into the corridor and, leaving the door open, leaned against the opposite wall. Poole stalked along the hall toward his office with the exaggerated dignity of the drunken man.

Fish conversed briefly and in whispers with his client, and Bob was disturbed to see the sudden light which flamed in Grubb's little eyes. He swore softly to himself. Fish was probably undoing all the good work he had accomplished. Presently the lawyer arose, slapped Pete encouragingly on the back, and left the room.

Bob went inside and closed the door. He did not say a word; simply sat down at the desk and with oil and rag went about carefully cleaning an already spotless sixgun. When he had finished his task, he noticed that the hunted look had returned to Pete Grubb's face.

The beginning of the trial was set for ten o'clock; at a few minutes before that hour his three deputies reported.

"They're fixin' to select the jury," said Deuce. "We figgered you might want to be in there. We can watch Mouldy for you."

Bob manacled Pete to the cot and locked the office door. "Watch from the corridor and you can keep yore eyes on the jail too. Don't let anybody upstairs. I'll be back in time to take Kurt Dodd and Pete into court."

He went downstairs and entered the court room, which was on the right side of the building. The place was packed, with men jammed about the doorways and along the walls. Judge Bleek was seated at the bench reading a newspaper; Poole and Fish were standing behind the railing facing several dozen men from among whom a jury was to be selected. Bob called the two lawyers to one side.

"I reckon there is no need to go very far with this,"

he said. "Pete Grubb is willin' to turn state's evidence. He'll go on the stand and tell the truth about the whole thing."

Poole exclaimed his astonishment; Fish simply nodded.

"The selection of the jury must go on just the same. Grubb's testimony must be heard and a verdict rendered. Where is he?"

"Locked in my office, with three deputies in the hall."

"Well, we can get along without your assistance, Sheriff. Your deputies may need you to help guard such a dangerous character."

The sneer decided Bob, as he afterward learned it was intended to do. He leaned against the railing. "I'll stick around and watch."

Absently he glanced out over the audience. Pop Purvis occupied a front seat, having gone without breakfast to secure it. Enright was there, as was Dutch Trumbauer and practically every cattleman within a radius of fifty miles. He saw Cole Bradshaw and the Kady crew. Dick was not with them, although Bob had seen him enter town in their company.

A group near the middle of the room caught his attention. It consisted of Tomlinson and his crutches, June, and Duke Haslam. Duke was carefully groomed and appeared serenely indifferent to the trial and its consequences. Occasionally he leaned over and spoke to June in an undertone. Bob could not judge whether or not his presence beside her was welcome. Tomlinson waved a huge hand at him, June smiled and nodded, and Haslam ignored him altogether.

The jury box was finally filled, the court called to order, and Thaddeus Poole, dignified, pompous, and considerably inebriated, turned to the bench.

"May it please the Court, since the indictment was returned an unexpected development has occurred in this case. The sheriff has informed me that one of the defendants, Peter Grubb, has expressed a desire to make a statement before this court. It is presumed that this statement will be in the nature of a confession. I am free to admit that without such a confession the County has no case. All the evidence which we are prepared to submit is circumstantial in its nature or based on the unsupported word of one man."

"I don't have to instruct you how to proceed," snapped Judge Bleek, who was suffering one of his "spells." "Have the sheriff bring in the defendants, read the charge against them, and put Grubb on the stand."

Poole turned to Bob. "Bring in your prisoners, Sheriff."

Outside the courthouse a volley of shots thundered and echoed, followed by the sound of voices raised in altercation. Bob, instantly apprehensive, ran through the doorway and down the corridor to the front entrance. Men swarmed about him, impeding his progress, shouting questions.

He reached the portico of the courthouse in time to see a body of horsemen riding down the street. Two of them appeared to be arguing violently, while some half-dozen others attempted to placate them. Bob recognized Shab Cannon and several others who had been in the park the day he was captured. The group appeared to be without evil intent; they rode slowly, and away from the jail. His fear of an attempted rescue vanished. Breathing a sigh of relief, he walked to the stairs which led to the second floor. Ace and Deuce were standing at the top, drawn sixguns in hand.

"What's goin' on down there?" asked the former.

"Some sort of argument. Don't know what about. Where's Joe?"

"We sent him back to reinforce the jailer in case anybody got the idea they were goin' to turn Kurt and Pete loose."

"Tell him to get Dodd and bring him to the court-room."

He found the key to his office, unlocked the door and flung it open. Then he stood on the threshold staring. A neat hole had been sawn in the board floor, and the prisoner was gone!

Bob swore and turned swiftly to Deuce. "Get Ace and come downstairs. Leave Dodd in the cell. Quick!"

The room immediately below his office was a store room. The door was locked, but they broke it down. Leading from it was a door opening into the Recorder's office, which, because of the trial, was deserted. From this another door opened on the alley behind the building. This door stood wide.

Bob reached it, stared out at the line of trees which fringed the creek, then turned to the crowd of men who had followed at his heels. "Get yore horses," he told them tersely, and ran toward the stable.

Despite his precautions they had bested him. For the past week men must have been working on the store-room ceiling, removing the lath and plaster at times when he and his prisoner were out of the office. The diversion before the courthouse had been staged to draw the guards to the head of the stairs at the far end of the corridor in order that the sound of a saw would not reach them. It had been very easy. One man could have liberated Grubb.

Bob swore softly. Haslam had been in the court room. So had Bradshaw. Shab was among the men in the street. The only absentee of any importance was Dick Markley. As Bob rode to the front of the building he saw Dick lounging against the door frame. He might have been among the spectators who could not get inside the building, or he might have gone from the store-room into the alley and circled the courthouse during the excitement.

Bob swiftly gathered his posse and divided it into several bands, dispatching them in different directions. The task was hopeless from the start. He returned to town that night weary and dejected. The other parties had already come in, equally unsuccessful. Frank Enright met him and clapped him on the back.

"It's just too bad," he said soberly. "None of us are blamin' you, Bob. Kurt is free. With most of the ones interested in convictin' him out lookin' for Pete, Thad Poole told the court the County was willin' to drop the case. They just turned Dodd loose."

Bob nodded and turned away to care for his tired horse. As he was riding to the stable, Duke Haslam and June came from the hotel. Duke was smiling, and blandly tipped his hat to Bob as they passed.

Bob dismounted at the stable and was loosening his latigo when Kurt Dodd came from the barn leading his horse. He stopped at sight of the sheriff, and Bob straightened in the savage hope that Dodd would go for his gun. Kurt's malevolence, however, manifested itself only in the flaming eyes and the words which rumbled from his heavy black beard.

"I told you I'd make you hard to find in this neck of the woods if I was turned loose, and by Godfrey! I meant it. Look to yoreself from now on, Bob Lee. There won't be no delay next time."

"Suits me," snapped Bob. "You're a liar and a thief and a killer. So are the rest of yore gang includin' Duke Haslam. I aim to put every one of you where you'll be quiet a long time."

At mention of Haslam's name, Dodd's eyes went wide, then narrowed again. He spoke through tight lips. "Now I know yore goose is cooked!"

He stared at Bob for several seconds, then nodded jerkily, stepped into his saddle, and rode away.

Chapter XIV

THE PROPOSAL

Bob ate a late supper and walked to the office. Ace, Deuce, and Joe were playing coon can, but stopped the game when he came in.

"Bob," asked Deuce, "who sawed that good-for-nothin' shrimp out?"

Bob shrugged and dropped into a chair. *"Quien sabe?"*

"Look here, Bob," said Ace seriously. "There ain't no use beatin' around the bush. You know who I figger done it? The same fella that Joe declares held up the stage, and the same one who lied when he said there was no fire in that park. Haslam was in the court room, and so was Bradshaw. Dodd was in jail, and you seen that red-headed Shab in the street; but where was Dick?"

"I saw him outside the courthouse right after I got my horse."

"Was he in the court room when the shootin' broke out?"

"No, but he might have been in the hall. A lot of men were."

"Uh-huh. But you didn't see him. Well, I figger he was the carpenter on the sawin' job. And I figger that he got Pete down the ladder we found in the store-room and hustled him out the back door and onto a horse."

Bob answered gloomily, "I hope for June's sake that you're wrong."

"I do too. Sometimes I wonder if she turned him down and soured him on the world."

"I don't think so. I believe she cares a lot for him."

"Then what in time does he want to go actin' like this for?" asked Deuce angrily. "Dang it! With a gal like that in love with a fella he shouldn't be able to do anything but go straight. Why, if it was me I'd—I'd—"

"Aw, go blow yore nose!" Ace told him. "You ain't got nerve enough to go crooked."

"If I ever do, my first act will be to ventilate a long-legged giraffe named Ace Talbot!"

"Me, I'm theenk Deek ees need money," said the sagacious Joe. "Haslam 'as bought heem, and now Deek ees w'at you call too deep from get out."

Bob stared at the Mexican; the same idea had occurred to him more than once. He dismissed the subject with a shrug. "Well, that's all water over the dam. The thing to do is plan for the next battle. Every one of that rustlin' outfit is free today, walkin' the streets, except Pete Grubb and they're takin' care of him. Like Deuce said, he's the weak sister of the outfit, and they saved him to prevent his squealin' on the stand."

"Well, what can we do?"

"Watch the range without letup. I heard them talkin' about a man named Vandervort who wants a thousand head of rustled cows. They'll make an effort to find them for him."

Deuce was skeptical. "After the way we busted up the other drive?"

"Yes. Kurt Dodd and Haslam are both tied to Lariat; they cain't change their field of operations. In the past they have done well. They just licked us in a court trial and are feelin' right cocky. Maybe they won't go at it on such a large scale, but you can bet they'll still rustle stock."

"But if we're watchin' them all the time—"

"We cain't watch every spread in the valley. And they'll work their cattle fast, handling them in small bunches. Tomorrow I'm goin' up county to look the ground over at Redrock. Pete had a deputy there and I don't know whether he's in the ring or not. I'll see him and talk with him. At the same time I'll try to get a line on this Vandervort. Ace, suppose you stay in town while I'm gone. Deuce, ride the north side of the valley, with headquarters at the Tumblin' T. Joe, you patrol the south side. We'll have to let the stage go for awhile."

They went outside, and while his deputies went after their horses, Bob strolled down to the Paris. Duke Haslam was seated at a table idly fingering a glass and smoking. Bob dropped into a chair opposite him and regarded him calmly.

Haslam smiled. "You had tough luck today, Lee. My condolences."

"Keep them. You're slick, Duke, but I aim to camp on yore trail until I get you dead to rights."

"Me? What have I to do with it?"

"Just about everything, I reckon. I've heard enough and seen enough to convince me that it was yore hand

that downed Rutherford, yore brain that planned the
stage and bank robberies, and yore decision that condemned me to death in the hills. I'm out to get you,
Duke. I aim to dig up enough evidence against you so
that even yore own besotted prosecutin' attorney and
dyspeptic judge will have to hand you over to me to
hang."

Haslam's face blackened. "It seems to me you're
talking too much with your mouth, young fellow. The
first thing you know you're going to make me mad,
and then you'll be sorry you didn't take my advice
about those wide-open spaces to the north, east, south,
and west."

Bob got to his feet. "I'm hopin' that some day I'll
make you mad enough to come out in the open and
quit operatin' through men and boys that yore money
has corrupted."

He left Haslam fuming and went over to the bar
where he had espied Dick Markley. Dick eyed him
apprehensively as he slipped in beside him, but Bob
spoke pleasantly and ordered two bottles of beer. When
they had finished drinking he said, "Dick, I wish you'd
come up to the office with me a minute. I got a proposition I want to talk over with you."

He saw the young man's eyes waver in Haslam's
direction. "What's it about, Bob?"

"Can't talk it over here; somethin' that will benefit
us both."

Dick eyed him doubtfully, then shrugged. "All right.
Lead on, Macduff."

They walked to Bob's office, and Lee lighted the
lamp on the desk. Both sat down and rolled cigarettes.

"Let her rip," said Dick.

Bob puffed thoughtfully for a minute. "Dick, I've been thinkin' about gettin' back into the cattle business."

Markley, who had expected the subject of the conversation to be along quite different lines, looked up interestedly. "Yeah?"

"Yes. The money I got from Tomlinson is lyin' idle in the bank. I want to put it to work. But as it is I'm tied up with this sheriff job for some time to come. So I got to thinkin' that if I could buy into some good outfit I might find somebody to look after my end for a share in the profits." Dick gave a start, but Bob hurried on. "For instance, suppose I gave you twenty thousand dollars with which to buy an interest in the Tumblin' T. You'd make out you were buyin' for yoreself, me bein' what you might call a silent partner. You'd keep half the profit, and I'd give you the option of buyin' me out when you'd made enough money to carry it alone. How does that strike you?"

Dick's voice was slightly choked. "Say that again, Bob."

"Shore. I give you twenty thousand and you buy an interest in the Tumblin' T. Half the profit is yores. Nominally you are Tomlinson's partner. When you save enough to swing the deal, you buy me out. That sets you up in business and lets me put my idle money to work. Easy enough, isn't it?"

"Too easy." Dick's eyes were bright. He got up and walked back and forth. "A share in the Tumblin' T; a chance to run my own iron and boss my own men; a decent livin' so that I can—" He broke off and came over to where Lee sat watching. "Bob, you old son-of-a-gun, I know why you're doin' this." His voice broke and for a moment he fought for control. "I know why you're doin' it, and I'm goin' to take yore offer. I'm ridin' out to the Tumblin' T tonight—now. Where's my hat?"

Bob grinned. "On yore head. I'm glad, Dick. And don't think I'm givin' you all the best of it. You'll make things hum on that spread."

When Dick had gone, Bob leaned back in his chair and relaxed. He had given the boy his chance. Dick would surely cut himself off from his vicious associates now, would plunge into the work of the ranch, would be in a position to ask June to marry him.

The light in Bob's eyes died, the softened lines of his face ironed out. Dick would marry June. That hurt; hurt like the devil. And yet, what else could he expect? Dick loved her and she loved him; they would be very happy together. And Bob, loving June as he did, could do no less than assure her the happiness to which she was entitled. But God! how it hurt.

The cigarette in his fingers burned out. He pinched it absently and dropped it on the floor. Slowly he got up and threw back his shoulders. He forced a grin. It was the only way. At least he had cheated Haslam; Dick was beyond his power now. The thought brought some measure of comfort.

Outside the Paris, Dick, about to swing into the saddle, stopped, removed his foot from the stirrup, and, glancing quickly about, pulled out his shirt and unbuckled Cole Bradshaw's money belt. With it doubled up in his hand he walked steadily into the saloon. Haslam was still at the table.

Dick strode quickly to him and dropped the money belt before him. "It's all there but thirty dollars," he said tersely. "I'll pay you that in a few days. I'm through, Duke, and this time neither you nor yore liquor can change me."

Duke looked up at him, his lip curling. "You'll squeal, I suppose?"

"I ought to slap yore face for that!"

"How about that confession?"

"Use it, and I'll drop you in yore tracks the first time I see you." He turned on his heel and walked out.

The distance to the Tumbling T never seemed longer; in reality, he covered it in probably quicker time than on the night of the bank robbery. He breathed a sigh of relief when he saw the light in the living room. As he swung off his horse, the door opened and June stood revealed in the yellow rectangle of light. Dick sprang up the steps and took both her hands.

"June, I got the greatest news for you! Bob told me to keep it to myself, but I got to tell you. Come over here and sit down." He urged her to a shadowed end of the gallery and almost forced her into a rocker. Dropping into a chair he hitched it close to hers, bent forward earnestly.

"June, he just made me an offer that almost bowled me over. He wants me to invest the money he got from yore dad for the ranch. Offered to let me have it to buy into yore dad's spread. Half the profit it to be mine. It means independence, a future, a chance to—

to tell you somethin' that otherwise I would have to keep to myself."

"Dick, that's wonderful. What a friend he is!"

"Ain't he, though! June, I don't know what to do. I've been wild and wicked and everything else, all because I needed money. I've stolen, I've double-crossed Bob, I've been everything I shouldn't. But that's past. That night I promised to go straight I went to—to the boss and told him I was through. He had somethin' he held over me, and talked me out of it. He cain't do it again. I told him so; dared him to do his worst."

"Dick, I'm proud of you. I knew you could do it. I wanted you to so much. Bob has stood by you staunchly, loyally. You'll never have another friend like him."

"I know it, and I feel very mean and awfully little. But that's gone now. I'm through. And June, all I did, wrong as it was, was for you. No, don't stop me! I loved you, June; loved you from the first moment I saw you in your father's camp with the firelight shinin' in yore hair. I knew then that I'd never be able to do without you. But as the days went by and I realized how little I had to offer you, I began to worry how I could make some money quick. I let this man I called the boss talk me into joinin' up with him. I was to get ten thousand dollars at the end of the year, and then I was to be free. June, I had to take it! Ten thousand dollars meant everything to me. And it was to be only for a year."

"Did you believe that? Did you believe he would release you?"

"What else could he do?"

"A moment ago you said he held something over you. Something that made you go on. Don't you see that at the end of the year he'd have had just that much more?"

"Yes, but he'd have to release me. If he didn't, well, I reckon I would have settled with him."

"And added murder to your other wrongdoings."

"It wouldn't have been murder. The man who kills him will be doin' a public service. But, as I said, that's over. He paid me a thousand dollars in advance; I returned it to him this evenin'. Tomorrow I'll come out and talk to yore father, and then—"

"Father will be glad to take you in with him," said June hastily. "He isn't old, but he needs a younger man to furnish the energy and drive."

"And can I work! June, girl, this old place will hum. And then, as I was goin' to say, after everything is settled, I'm goin' to ask you to make things complete by—marryin' me."

"Dick!"

"Shore! Didn't I tell you that I've been in love with you ever since I've seen you? Of course, it's only been a couple of weeks, but I figure that when a fella meets the one woman he don't need to know her for six years to find it out. No, sir, I didn't. And June, honey—"

"Dick—please!" The distress in her voice halted him. He reached out and took her hand. She was trembling.

"Why, June honey, what's the matter? You do love me, don't you? Why, shucks! You took up for me, and you encouraged me, and you stuck by me and refused to tell what a skunk I was! Why—why—June, girl, you *do* love me, don't you?"

"Dick, you make it so difficult!"

"What do you mean?"

"I like you; I do indeed! And I am interested in you; I want you to go straight, and I'd like to think that I had helped you. But, Dick, I can't marry you. I wish I could! I wish I cared for you in the way you want me to, but I don't."

"You—don't—love me?" Dick appeared to be stunned.

"Not that way, Dick. Oh, I'm sorry if I gave you the impression that I did! I tried to help you for Bob's sake. It was such a pity to see your fine friendship spoiled. He believed in you, Dick, and I wanted you to be worthy of his loyalty. I thought that if you had made a misstep perhaps you would realize it before it was too late. I tried to help—to encourage."

Dick's voice was husky. "And you did—what you did—for Bob."

"Yes."

"You love him."

"I always have, Dick."

Markley got to his feet and stood, lean and rigid, before her. "He tricked me then! Sent me here to make a fool of myself!"

"That isn't so. He doesn't know how I feel toward him. For all I know he doesn't care for me at all. Please, Dick, let's be sensible. Take this opportunity that Bob has offered you; take it and make good. I'll be your friend; I'll help all I can."

"Friend!" Dick's laugh was short, bitter. "That's

usually what the girl offers her rejected suitors, ain't it? Friend! No, I won't take his offer. How could I? To be near you every day; to see you—talk with you, always rememberin' that I must keep my hand from touchin' yores, look at you like you were my sister, act like it didn't matter whether you were near me or a mile away! No, I won't take his offer."

June got to her feet and put her hands firmly on his shoulders. "Dick, listen to me. If you don't feel like buying in with father, speak with Mr. Enright or Mr. Trumbauer. Buy in somewhere. If you value my love so highly isn't my friendship, my respect, worth something? Dick, tell me that it is; tell me that you're through with this wild, irresponsible life. There are other girls far worthier of your love than I. In time—"

"Not in ten thousand years! There'll never be another for me."

"Dick, I'm terribly sorry."

"Don't go to pityin' me. I hate pity. I ain't the first one got the mitten." He turned away, but she grasped him by an arm and held him.

"Not that way, Dick. Tell me you're not angry; promise that you'll go straight. Please!"

Dick's face was stony. "I'll promise nothin'. I'm done with promises. From now on I live my life in my own way." He turned, went down the steps, and, flinging himself into the saddle, spurred his horse to a fast run.

Straight to the Kady he headed, jaw set, eyes hard and cold. He was mortally hurt, stabbed to the quick; for once in his willful life he had been brought up short on the very verge of achievement, and his reaction was one of stubborn, reckless resentment.

At the Dodd ranch he was challenged, recognized, and passed. He flung himself from his horse and strode into the front room. Duke Haslam, Kurt Dodd, Cole Bradshaw, and Shab Cannon were seated around a table.

Haslam spoke quietly. "Hello, Dick. Change yore mind?"

Dick crossed the floor, took a bottle from the mantel and drank long and deeply. Putting it back he turned to the table.

"What's in the wind?" he asked coldly.

"Plenty," answered Haslam. "I'll tell you about it. And while I think of it—" He drew the money belt from his pocket and dropped it on the table.

CHAPTER XV

THE LION AND THE RAT

B OB rode to Redrock on the day following his conversation with Dick. He looked up Grubb's deputy and found him a lazy, shifty-eyed fellow eminently fitted by nature to hang over a bar or shoot pool. Bob determined to replace him at the earliest possible moment. The third day saw him back in Lariat, where he found Ace yawning over a game of solitaire. The tall cowboy expressed such an earnest desire to join Deuce at the Tomlinson spread that Bob gave him permission to go.

"By the way," he asked casually, "have you seen anything of Dick?"

"Nope, and I don't care if I never do. Bob, that lad's comin' to a bad end. Some men are born to be hung, and I reckon Dick's one of them."

"Some men are born strong and some weak. Generally the weak ones are the most likable. Dick is one of them. If it hadn't been for Duke Haslam Dick would still be the happy-go-lucky cowboy we used to know."

"Well, mebbe you're right; but I always figgered that when a fella takes the crooked path he does it with his eyes open and deserves what he gets."

"You speak the way you do because you happen to have been born strong instead of weak. Also you haven't been as close to Dick as I have. There isn't a more courageous lad on the range. He dragged me out of an arroyo brimmin' with flood water after a chunk of driftwood had knocked me unconscious. When he jumped in there didn't appear to be a Chinaman's chance for either of us, but he jumped in just the same. A fella doesn't forget things like that in a hurry, Ace."

Ace nodded sober agreement. "Reckon it's the same with me and Deuce. . . . Well, I'll be ramblin'. Didn't find out anything about that fella Vandervort, did you?"

"Not a thing; but I had to be right cautious."

"Uh-huh. Ask Pop Purvis. If anybody around here knows it'll be him."

Bob followed the suggestion within the hour. Pop was seated, as usual, on the veranda of the hotel. Bob dropped into a chair beside him, and after a few interchanges of commonplaces asked him if he had seen Dick lately.

"The joker? Nope, I ain't. Bob, that fella got me guessin'. If he's workin' for you, you shore are playin' a slick game; if he ain't, I'd look out for him."

"Enright or Trumbauer been in town?"

"Both of 'em. That there Dutch is a funny fella, ain't he?"

"Odd name—Trumbauer."

"I've heard odder ones. There was old man Heffle— Heffledingle. I always have to take two whacks at that name to say it. Good old fella, too."

"I heard á strange one the other day. Vanderbart, or somethin' like that."

"Vanderbart? Reckon you mean Vandervort. He's

from Holland—or his folks are. Owns the Flyin' V across the line in Texas. Don't know him personal, but I've heard of him."

Bob talked awhile longer, then got up and went to the office. "So Vandervort is over the line in Texas," he mused. "That means any stuff they deliver to him must go through the Bottle Neck. And I'll bet a good horse against a Mex *peso* they'll try to deliver some. But they'll have to handle them like hot pennies; cain't take the chance of holdin' any in the hills while worked-over brands heal. Would they drive with the original brands on them? Answer: they would, if they were Tumblin' T's. Why? Because the Tumblin' T is not yet registered in the brand books of this state."

He sat there for a long time following this train of thought, and when at last the growing dusk warned him that the supper hour was near, he had a pretty clear idea of how the enemy would go about gathering and driving Vandervort's order. He rode immediately to the Tumbling T. Ace and Deuce had gone out on range patrol, but Tomlinson and his daughter were in the living room.

"Mr. Tomlinson," he said after greetings had been exchanged, "I sort of figured some things out while I was in the office today. Pop Purvis identified this man Vandervort for me, and I believe I see just how they aim to fill that order of his, you to supply the cows." He went on to explain.

"Sounds reasonable," agreed Tomlinson. "What do you aim to do?"

"Furnish the rope to hang them. To begin with, when the boys come in tomorrow send them to town.

I'll ride over to the other side of the valley and round up Joe. We'll let them while away a few days in McGarvey's Pool Parlour. You can tell yore crew to be kind of careless about checkin' up the cattle near that spring which is so close to the Kady."

"How will you know when they've rustled the stock? They're apt to slip a bunch out on us before we can stop them."

"We'll know," said Bob cryptically, and got up to go.

June walked with him as far as the gallery.

"Have you seen Dick lately?" he asked her.

"Not since a few nights ago. He rode out to tell me of the proposition you made him. Bob, it was splendid of you."

"I thought I'd sold him on the idea; I've been wonderin' what became of him."

For a short space June stood beside him pensively gazing into the shadows. Her conversation with Dick had been so intimate that she shrank from relating it to Bob. "I don't know where he went," she said at last.

"I see. Well, good-night, Miss June."

"Good-night, Bob." She stood watching as he swung into the saddle and vanished into the darkness.

Just a week after this conversation, the north-bound stage, which usually reached Lariat by sundown, pulled in late. Instead of continuing to the stage station, the driver pulled up at the courthouse and Bob, who had just finished his supper, heard his shouted inquiry as to the whereabouts of the sheriff. Bob immediately presented himself.

"What do you want?"

"Holdup," announced the driver briefly. "Just this side of Redrock. Three masked men. They shot my messenger, took the strong box, and robbed the passengers. I turned back to Redrock with the messenger, then came on through."

"What time did it happen?"

"This mornin' around ten."

"Get a description of the men?"

"They were masked, but one was short and chunky and wore a calfskin vest. Another was tall. Couldn't see nothin' much but his eyes. They were gray—and mean. He's the jasper that shot Simmons. The third was medium height, dark hair—"

"Where did they hold you up and which way did they go?"

"At the four corners this side of Redrock. They was ridin' the same direction as we were, with their backs to us. As we overtook them, two pulled off to one side of the road and the third one to the other side. We didn't think a thing of it, but as we were passin', one of them turned his head and Simmons seen he had a mask on. He raised his shotgun and the fella plugged him. One covered me and the other two got down the strong box and lined up the passengers. They rode east."

"I'll round up my deputies and start after them."

Bob thought the thing over as he hurried toward the Pool Parlour where the boys had gone after supper. The hour for action had struck; this holdup was the bait which was intended to draw him from Lariat. The short chunky man was Shab Cannon; the tall lean one, Cole Bradshaw. There was no doubt in Bob's mind as to the identity of the third. It was Dick Markley.

He found his three deputies, curtly summoned them, and spent a precious half hour in purchasing supplies and making up blanket rolls. They rode out of Lariat at a brisk canter, Duke Haslam forming one of the idle crowd which witnessed their hurried departure.

A mile or so outside of town Bob waved farewell, and, in accordance with the prearranged plan, swung across the range. The three deputies continued their way with instructions to attempt to run down the stage bandits. Joe was to ride back later and report.

At the Tumbling T Bob assembled the crew and ordered them to saddle up. He talked the thing over briefly with June, Tomlinson, and the Tumbling T foreman. "We'll cut across the pass above the Kady and ride to the Bottle Neck. We've plenty of time. I figure they won't start the drive until tomorrow mornin', aimin' to drive through the Neck and bed down in the valley tomorrow night. We'll be there when they come through. Let's ride."

He gave June no opportunity to speak with him alone, reluctant to reveal the identity of the third man in the holdup. By the bleak look in her eyes he judged that she had guessed the truth, and the knowledge hurt him.

Midnight found the little posse climbing the grade to the pass; by dawn they had reached the valley on the far side of the hills. Here they spent an hour in eating breakfast and resting their horses. Late in the afternoon they halted at the mouth of the Bottle Neck, a cautious scout by Bob having convinced him that the pass was unguarded.

The foreman and three of his men were dispatched across the mouth of the gap with instructions to find shelter among the rocks with which the place was littered. Bob remained on the near side with the remaining two cowboys. Thus the drive, after emerging from the Bottle Neck, would be forced to pass between the two forces.

Time passed. The sun disappeared and twilight fell swiftly. Bob's men lounged on the ground, smoking and talking. Bob sat near them, outwardly placid, inwardly restless and apprehensive. The gray of twilight was succeeded by the mauve of approaching darkness; objects became indistinct, then gradually assumed new ghostlike form as the moon came up. With a word to his men, Bob tightened the cinches and, mounting, rode into the Bottle Neck.

On the far side of the passage he halter in the shadow of some rocks and sat listening. At first he could hear nothing but the usual small noises of the night, then came the low muffled thud of hoofs, the faint occasional bawl of a complaining steer. He jerked erect in the saddle and wheeled his horse. The drive was approaching!

The rustlers were behind schedule, and the darkness necessitated a change in plan. Joining the group on the far side of the Neck, Bob tersely instructed them in the part they were to play, then, returning to his two men, he repeated the instructions for their benefit. Tense with expectancy they climbed into their saddles and sat waiting in the shadows.

The noise of the moving cattle reached them, then, looming ghostlike in the moonlight, the vanguard rode out of the pass. Bob counted six men at the head of the column. Once in the open, four of the six left their places, two taking stations on each side of the herd. Here they sat watching as the cattle shuffled by. They were swing riders, and Bob presently saw one of the two on his side turn his horse and ride on the flank of the cattle, leaving his companion to care for the rear half of the herd.

With a whispered word to his companions, Bob reined his horse and, hoofbeats drowned by the noise of the cattle, circled and cut to the edge of the herd behind the first swing man. At the sound of horse's hoofs behind him the rustler reined in and turned in his saddle.

"Whadda you want?" he called, mistaking Bob for one of his own men.

Bob raised his arm in an indefinite gesture and drew up beside him. Not until then did the other recognize him.

"Pull off to one side," ordered Bob, his sixgun nudging the other's ribs. "And don't make any mistakes. Quick!"

The fellow stared for a moment, then with a curse of astonishment, obediently reined away from the drive. Back among the boulders Bob disarmed him, and, making him dismount, bound and gagged him. The horse was securely tied to a stunted pine.

Without a flank rider to keep them in formation the

animals were beginning to leave the column. Bob struck diagonally for the head of the herd, knowing that his two Texans would take care of the other swing man on his side. If the plan was working according to schedule, the four Tumbling T cowboys on the opposite side could be depended upon to seize the flankers there. The two rustlers at the point must be captured before the drag passed through the Bottle Neck.

Bob did not attempt a cautious approach. Cutting swiftly around the edge of the lead steers he called, "Come here!" to one of the men. The fellow reined about and trotted his horse toward Bob.

"What's the matter with you dudes?" the rustler shouted. "The danged critters are scatterin' all over the flat."

Bob jumped his horse forward and as the other pulled up in surprise the threatening sixgun covered him.

"Come along, and not a peep out of you."

For a brief moment the fellow hesitated; then he raised his voice in a warning shout and reached for his gun. Bob jumped his horse forward again and made two desperate swipes with his gun. The first knocked the other's weapon from his hand; the second caught him on the side of the head and sent him spinning from the saddle. This man, too, was secured and dragged behind the rocks.

By this time the herd was disintegrating, and since he felt reasonably sure that the second point man had been captured by the boys on the far side of the herd, Bob returned to the place where he had left his own men. He found them cheerfully smoking, the second swing rider lying on the ground neatly bound.

"I'm goin' to work in behind the drag," Bob told them. "Two of the boys on the other side will do the same. You watch this end, and don't let anybody through."

They nodded and ground their cigarettes in the dust. Bob started threading among the rocks, keeping to the shadows and as close to the wall of the Neck as was possible. Presently he heard voices and reined in, listening.

"What's wrong with them flank men! They've let the whole danged herd get away from them!" The angry speaker was Kurt Dodd.

A quavering voice answered, pitched high to carry above the noise of the traveling cattle. "It's a trick, I betcha! That Lee jigger has coppered our bet. Kurt, I told you he would."

"You're loco. Lee's at Redrock. Some lousy son has gone to sleep."

"I tell you it's a trick! Kurt, I'm goin' back."

"You're stayin' right here!" thundered Dodd. "By cripes, if it's a trick you take yore chances with the rest of us."

"I won't! I tell you I'm goin' back! We was crazy to try this right after what happened. I told you we was. I'm goin'—"

The sullen boom of a sixgun interrupted him. Bob heard a shriek of agony, short, horrible in its significance.

"Served the damned rat right," came another voice.

"He was all primed to squeal. Come on, Kurt; let's see what's wrong up front."

Bob heard the quickened thud of hoofs, caught a brief glance of a half-dozen men riding through the gap. He spurred quickly in the opposite direction, dragging his rifle from its sheath at the same time. Half way through the pass he halted and reined about. The moon, directly above, lighted the passage dimly, but the dust made it impossible to distinguish friend from foe.

The whiplike crack of a rifle sounded to his right, followed by a volley of revolver shots and a chorus of hoarse yells. Another rifle spat—a third—a fourth; then a veritable crash of furious gun fire echoed the length of the pass.

Hoofs thundered, and four men came tearing along the moonlit strip headed back toward the safety of the hills. Bob threw his rifle to his shoulder and fired. A horse stumbled and fell. Rifles cracked on the opposite side, and a rider pitched from the saddle. The remaining two continued their headlong flight. One lay stretched along his horse's neck; the other rode upright, huge, defiant, unafraid.

Again Bob fired and missed; the two rifles blazed from the far side of the pass and also missed; then the two riders were directly between them and neither party dared fire for fear of hitting the other.

Slipping the rifle back into its boot, Bob spurred out into the pass, angling for a point some distance ahead of the two men. Swift to take the cue, a horseman flashed from the shadows across the pass.

Despite their speed, both pursuers were forced to

fall in behind the fleeing rustlers; but Bob's companion, who still carried his rifle, halted his horse and raised the weapon. He sighted for a moment, then pulled the trigger, and one of the horses fell in a heap, shot through and through. The rider pitched headlong and lay still. Bob raced after the remaining outlaw, who still rode stiffly erect, defiantly presenting a broad back to his pursuer.

Unexpectedly the rustler's horse slipped, recovered its balance, tried gamely to regain its stride; but the animal limped, and the distance between pursued and pursuer decreased rapidly. Bob was a bare fifty feet behind when the other reined in and wheeled his horse. The moonlight shone full on the heavy, bearded face, and Bob recognized Kurt Dodd. Instantly he slid his own mount to a stop, and for a brief moment the two men gazed at each other less than twenty feet apart.

Dodd's face was granite hard, his eyes glittered like black beads. Both fired at the same time, guns whipping up and bellowing in unison. Bob heard the angry whine of a slug, and a lock of his hair moved as though disturbed by a puff of wind. He fired again.

Dodd jerked almost imperceptibly, swayed, reached for the saddle horn with his left hand. Bob, tense thumb holding back the hammer of his gun, watched while the outlaw tried vainly to raise his six-shooter for another shot. The will was strong, but strength had gone from the brawny arm. The hammer slipped from beneath Kurt's thumb and the bullet struck a stone and whined away into the moonlight. Then Dodd's bearded head drooped, his figure went slack, and he slipped inertly from the saddle to lay in a grotesque position, one foot caught in the stirrup.

Bob dismounted and, releasing the foot, stretched Dodd out on the ground. He had a canteen of water on his saddle and forced some of it between the stricken man's lips. Another rider came up at a run, but his arm was in the air and Bob finally recognized the foreman of Tomlinson's men.

"Got him, huh?" the Texan remarked as he swung from the saddle. "I stopped to tie up the fella I ditched." He bent over and examined Dodd. "Got him through the chest. Well, he won't rustle no more cows."

Dodd opened his eyes and looked up at them. Bob knelt beside him.

"Kurt, you're goin' to cash," he said quietly. "Better go out clean. I got a witness here. Tell the truth: who was behind the shootin' of John Rutherford?"

Kurt gazed steadily up at him, and his eyes, which had dulled, blazed once more. He struggled to speak, and a little bloody froth appeared on his lips. The words came slowly, painfully.

"You go—to hell!"

The big form stiffened, the eyes glazed. Kurt Dodd was dead.

Tomlinson's foreman sighed. "Some folks are awful contrary. . . . Well, let's mosey back and see if they's any more chores to be done."

On the way back they met another rider. He proved to be the one who had accompanied the foreman to the middle of the pass. "All over," he told them laconically. "The boys at the mouth downed two, there's two more cussin' their luck in the middle of the Neck,

and if you fellas got yores, that accounts for them all."
He flexed his muscles and added cheerfully, "I'd say
a nice time was had by all."

In the middle of the gap they found the body of
Pete Grubb. He had been shot while attempting to flee.
Tomlinson's foreman stirred him with the toe of a boot,
contemptuously.

"He was just what that fella called him: a rat. Just
a common, ord'nary, sneakin' little rat. And Dodd—
well, I reckon you could call him a lion and not miss
it by much."

CHAPTER XVI

DEUCE WINS THE TOSS

SHORTLY after noon of the next day an unexpected procession entered Lariat. At its head rode three men who sagged weakly in their saddles. Each led a horse on which was tied the body of a dead rustler. Behind these rode a group of six disgruntled captives, and bringing up in the rear were three of Tomlinson's cowboys and Sheriff Bob Lee.

Bob halted the party before the courthouse, ordered the six sound prisoners from their horses, and, calling upon two of Tomlinson's men to help him, herded them into the building and locked them in cells. Men surrounded Bob as he returned to the street, asking eager questions; but he told them he would give them the story later, and proceeded to conduct his three wounded captives to the office of Doc Weatherspoon. He left two of his companions to guard them while their injuries were being dressed, instructed the other to put the captured horses in the jail corral, and continued down the street with the remaining three animals and their gruesome burdens.

He found the proprietor of the undertaking establishment awaiting him, and, dismounting, busied himself untying the knots which held the dead outlaws in their saddles. A sudden sharp exclamation sounded at his elbow, and he turned swiftly to look into the face of Duke Haslam.

The owner of the Paris had been shocked out of his calm. His face was deathly white, his eyes burning. The dead rustlers were draped over their horses in such positions that Haslam could not see their faces. He nodded jerkily. "Who are they?" he asked.

"One was called 'Gloomy'; I don't know his real name. The others are Pete Grubb and Kurt Dodd."

"Kurt!" There was agony in the blurted word, and Bob realized with some surprise that Haslam was deeply affected.

"Tried to drive a bunch of Tumblin' T steers through the Bottle Neck. We were layin' for them and trapped them. Haslam, I'm goin' to tie you up with this bunch yet. You might like to know that Kurt died game. He knew he was goin', but he wouldn't squeal. He shot Pete to keep him from talkin'."

For a moment it appeared as if Haslam had lost his nerve; then, quite suddenly, he stiffened and the flame leaped into his eyes again.

"Damn you, Lee!" he said in a low, tense voice. "I'll get you for this if it's the last thing I do!" Before Bob could reply he had turned and was walking through the crowd, brushing men roughly from his path in his blind haste.

Bob helped the undertaker carry the bodies into his parlors, then told the curious crowd briefly what had happened. Excitement turned to adulation and he had a difficult time getting away. He finally made his escape with the horses, removed the equipment, and put them in the corral. The wounded men arrived in the company of their guards and were locked up, after which Bob and the Tumbling T men descended upon a restaurant and ordered double portions of steak, hashed brown potatoes, coffee, bread pudding, and apple pie.

The meal finished, Tomlinson's men started back toward the ranch, and Bob spent an unprofitable afternoon trying to wring information from prisoners who were determined not to talk. They were disgruntled and sullen; none seemed to remember for whom they were working, and all appeared to resent the fact that Bob had been at the Neck when he was supposed to be in Redrock.

He was on his way to supper when Joe Villegas rode in on a lathered pony. The Mexican dropped wearily from his saddle and stumbled across the sidewalk to where Bob had halted.

"I'm mos' dead from slip," he apologized. "We ride lak 'ell from tam we get to Redrock."

"Any luck?"

Joe shrugged. "We 'ave not'ing to go on except they ride east. Eees lak look from needle in smokestack."

"I reckon so. Well, what do you want to do first; eat or sleep?"

"Me, I'm 'ongry. I'm can eat two, t'ree cow."

"All right. Come along to the hotel with me. I'll ride to Redrock in the mornin'. You stay in town and hold down the office. We got nine prisoners caught in the act of rustlin' cows, and they all seem to think that Sylvester Fish is goin' to save their necks for them." Bob told him the story while he cared for Joe's horse. At the conclusion the Mexican swore softly.

"Seven men keel t'ree, woun' t'ree, and mak the prisoner of seex! Ees good job, *amigo*."

"The seven were Texas men, Joe."

"Ees mak difference," Joe admitted loftily. "May be those pipples from Redrock fin' out w'at Texas men can do. Ace and Deuce they ride out of town weeth me. They t'ink the t'ree 'oldup men come back eef they mak out lak they ride to Lariat."

"Not a bad idea," said Bob.

He left for Redrock the next morning, not dreaming that he was riding into tragedy. Before starting he searched all the prisoners again and went over every inch of their cells. Joe was instructed to permit nobody to see the prisoners during his absence. Two day men and a night jailer were on hand to assist the Mexican.

While Bob was holding to a trail gait on his way to Redrock, his two deputies in that neighborhood were camped on the side of a hill which overlooked the little town. Since noon of the day before they had doggedly held their positions, alternating in watching.

Toward evening of the first day they had seen a horseman leave Redrock, and had identified him as the shifty-eyed former deputy of Pete Grubb.

"It shore is amazin' how far that Duke Haslam's arm can reach," observed Ace. "I don't like the looks of that jigger down there, and I'll bet six bits against a lead nickel that he's ridin' right now to tell Shab and Cole and Dick that we're on our way to Lariat."

"I shore hope he does. I'm honin' for action. Bob, back there at the Bottle Neck, is hoggin' all the fun while we mess around hills lookin' for three jiggers that rode east a half day before. East! My gosh; they could be in Georgia now."

"You ain't loco enough to think they'll keep travelin' east, are you? Betcha if they come back it'll be from the south. That's the way this jigger just rode."

The rest of the afternoon dragged without sign of the three bandits, or, for that matter, of the rider who had left town several hours before. With the approach of darkness the two deputies left their camp and descended to the neighborhood of the town. Separating, one circled Redrock to station himself near the road which entered the village from the south, while the other took a position near the one which led from the north.

Their vigil was in vain, and with the setting of the moon they joined forces and returned to their hill camp for a few hours' sleep.

"If this keeps up very long we'll have to give it up as a bad job or show our hand by ridin' to town for supplies," said Deuce as they munched a cold breakfast. "Betcha that jigger just rode out to see his sick grandma."

Ace agreed somberly and stretched out on the edge of the cliff to resume his watch of the town. Almost immediately he reported to Deuce. "That jigger you just mentioned is ridin' back to town. Comin' from the south."

"His grandma must 'a' got well again," murmured Deuce.

Mid-morning brought the north-bound stage. It stopped at Redrock for a few minutes, then lumbered out of town on its way to Lariat. The dust of its passage had hardly settled when Ace called Deuce to him.

"Look! To the south there. Three riders. See 'em?"

Deuce squinted against the bright light. "Shore. Three of 'em, or I'm a Chinaman! Big boy, let's get goin'."

They discussed plans while they saddled their horses.

"Comin' in for supplies," said Deuce. "That means they're headin' for the store. Ace, how'll we tackle 'em? Ride right in a-shootin'?"

"We'd likely scare them off or get plugged ourselves. There's three to our two, and they can all shoot."

"We could come in from opposite ends of the street."

"Then we'd be pluggin' at each other."

"Yeah, that's right. You'd probably hit me; especially if you was aimin' at somethin' else. How about you takin' one alley and me the other? One of us could walk in the back door of the store while the other covered the front."

"Deuce, sometimes you amaze me by showin' symptoms of intelligence. I'll take the alley behind the store and do the walkin' in on 'em."

"You will not. You'd likely butt yore brains out on the top of the door frame and save 'em the trouble of shootin' you. I'll do the walkin' in."

"You ain't big enough to see over a counter. They'd pepper you while you was huntin' for a box to stand on."

"If I'm that little they'd have a hard time hittin' me at all."

"And if I'm so danged skinny like you say, I could walk sideways and they couldn't even see me."

Deuce fished a quarter from his pocket. "We'll toss for it. Heads, I take the back door; tails, you take it." He flipped the coin. "Heads she is. There must be a special Providence guidin' this affair. You'd be shore to make a mess of it."

"Aw, you make me tired! When you get in there shoot 'em; don't try to talk them to death."

Cautiously they descended to the floor of the valley, seeking every bit of cover so as to avoid being seen by the approaching horsemen. They followed the low spots until they were back of the town. Here it was necessary that Ace circle in order to reach the alley behind the row of buildings on the far side of the street.

Deuce dismounted and tied his horse to a cedar, then made his way to the rear of the store, keeping the building between himself and anyone who might happen to be on the town's single street. He reached the alley in safety and cautiously peered around a corner of the building.

Presently he heard the measured thud of hoofs, and three men rode into view. His heart gave a leap as he recognized Shab Cannon, Cole Bradshaw, and Dick Markley. They were not wearing masks.

They passed out of Deuce's range of vision, and he heard the creak of leather as they swung from their saddles in front of the store. Boots clumped across the sidewalk and up the wooden steps.

Deuce hesitated. Ace had not had sufficient time to reach his position, but to delay very long meant that the three would be bunched in front of the store when the two deputies made their play. Reasoning that Ace would abandon caution and come at a run if he heard a shot, Deuce drew his gun, examined it briefly, more from habit than necessity, and stepped to the rear door.

He raised the latch and pulled. The door swung back noiselessly. Deuce, peering through a crack, saw that it opened behind a pile of merchandise which hid it from those at the front of the store. He slipped through the opening, closed the door carefully, and tiptoeing to the pile of merchandise peered over it. Shab was at the counter and Cole Bradshaw stood in the doorway.

"A sack of flour," ordered Shab.

The storekeeper nodded and started for the rear of the store. Deuce swore under his breath. The merchandise behind which he was hiding consisted of sack upon sack of flour!

A dozen paces from him, the storekeeper halted, staring. Vainly Deuce signaled for silence. In the gloom the man did not recognize him.

"Come out of that!" he snapped. "Who are you?"

Both Shab and Bradshaw tensed, their hands flashing to guns.

Deuce leaped from behind the sacks. "Put 'em up!"

Neither man obeyed. Shab, cursing, fired, the report blending with that of Deuce's gun. Deuce felt a searing blow on his left thigh at the same instant he saw the dust spurt from the calfskin vest. Shab uttered a hoarse bellow and staggered backward, still thumbing his hammer. The slugs went wild, but close enough for Deuce to hear their vicious scream. He fired again, saw the dust spurt from the calfskin vest once more.

Bradshaw, at the door, had had no chance to shoot because Shab stood between him and the deputy. Now he leaped forward as Shab was about to collapse, and, circling him with his left arm, started pumping lead at Deuce. A heavy slug struck Deuce on the shoulder with terrific impact and knocked him down. When he tried to raise his gun his arm muscles refused to obey his will.

Quickly he reached over with his left hand and plucked the weapon from his numbed fingers. Another bullet struck him, but he was unaware of any pain. The smoke almost completely hid the two men from him. He raised his weapon with his left arm and fired until it was empty.

Outside he heard the sound of a shot, then the frenzied voice of Dick Markley, "Through the back door, fellas!" Came the thud of hoofs, the rumble of planks as the horses were urged across the sidewalk, Dick's voice repeating, "Out the back way, fellas! Out the back way!"

Shab's body thumped on the floor and Cole Bradshaw came leaping out of the smoke pall. His eyes were cold and glittering, and a thin line of smoke eddied from the muzzle of his gun. He glanced down at Deuce, leveled the Colt swiftly, and snapped the hammer. It fell on an empty shell and Bradshaw, with a wicked oath, leaped over Deuce, wrenched open the door, and sprang into the saddle on his waiting horse.

Deuce heard him yell, "Shab's down. Cut his horse loose and ride!" Then came the swift staccato pound of hoofs.

Ace stumbled through the smoke-filled doorway. He

was yelling, "Deuce! Where are you, you li'l' runt? Answer me, dang you!"

"I'm—here," gasped Deuce. "Stop—yore bellerin'. And don't—step on me—with them—big feet."

Ace came striding across the floor and dropped on his knees beside his partner. "Where you hit, buddy?"

The little cowboy's face was a sickly white, but he grinned. "Danged if I know. Three—four places. Ace, Cole—forgot—his flour."

When Ace picked him up he fainted.

Bob arrived an hour later. Deuce was still unconscious, and a grim-faced Ace sat beside the cot on which he lay, bathing the still face with cold water, replacing the blood-soaked bandages. There was no doctor at Redrock.

Tersely he told Bob of the fight. "The li'l' runt would have to take the most dangerous part," he complained bitterly. "I oughtn't 'a' let him do it. Likely he cheated me on that toss just to get it." For a moment he was sielnt, then he looked somberly at Bob. "I'll get Cole Bradshaw for this."

"The first thing to do is get Deuce to Lariat," said Bob. "I'll dig up a spring wagon and some mattresses. The road is good and we can get him there in about the time it would take to bring Doc Witherspoon here. You start after Bradshaw. I'll be back to help just as soon as I can make it."

"Take him to the Tumblin' T," suggested Ace. "It ain't much farther and the li'l' runt would want to be there."

Bob nodded and went after the wagon. Shortly after noon he started the long, slow trip to Lariat.

Chapter XVII

CORNERED

JOSÉ VILLEGAS sat at the desk in the sheriff's office tranquilly smoking. It was mid-afternoon, and José had been sitting there almost continually since Bob had left for Redrock. The office door was open, and from his position Joe was able to see into the corridor and, consequently, any one who attempted to reach the cells to which it led. Thus far the job had been a dull, uninteresting one; but Joe had determined that his chief's instructions would be carried out to the full.

Somebody ascended the stairs at the front of the building, and Joe sat up expectantly; but the footsteps died as the person entered an office at that end of the hall, and Joe relaxed once more. Presently the footsteps sounded again, and this time they were undoubtedly approaching. Furthermore, Joe decided that the one man had now become two.

He got up from his chair and gliding softly to the doorway leaned against the frame. The two were Thaddeus Poole and Sylvester Fish. They would have passed Joe without noticing him had he not said softly, almost apologetically, "One moment, *señores*."

They halted, and the prosecuting attorney turned to survey him. "Oh, it's you. We were going back to the jail."

Joe smiled gently. "That ees not permit'."

"Oh, yes it is," contradicted the pompous Poole. "Mr. Fish is the legal adviser of the men who are being held."

"Ees mak no difference. She can not go back."

Poole fixed a cold hard eye upon the Mexican. "I shall have to instruct you, sir, in the ethics of jurisprudence."

Joe bore up bravely under this. "I'm not spik ver' good *Ingles*," he explained. "May be you don't too, eh?"

The brick red of Poole's cheeks deepened. He turned curtly to his companion. "No use arguing with this fellow, Sylvester. I will accompany you."

He started again for the jail section of the courthouse, but halted abruptly as the muzzle of Joe's gun prodded him in the ribs.

"I'm say eet ees not permit' that you go to the jail. The sheriff she tell me nobody ees to see these men until she return."

"Why that is ridiculous! I tell you this man is their lawyer; he has a perfect right to speak with his clients."

"W'en the sheriff return, may be she weel geeve the permission. Until then," Joe shrugged expressively, "ees toff lock."

Fish exclaimed his irritation. "I'll fix him, Thad. I'll get an order from Bleek. Come on." They turned and walked down the corridor to Judge Bleek's office. Joe shifted his weight and hummed a little tune.

In a short while they back back again, this time

triumphantly waving a paper before Joe's eyes. "Now maybe you'll let us pass," snapped Fish.

"W'at ees eet?" asked Joe blandly.

"It's a court order authorizing me to visit my clients. Read it."

Joe glanced indifferently at the paper. "I'm mos' sorry, but I'm not read the *Ingles*."

"A fine deputy you are! Can't even read English. Well, I'll read it for you. It says—"

"Ees no matter." Joe dismissed the whole affair with a wave of the hand. "You are not permit' to enter."

"Why you ignorant fool!" blazed Fish. "Do you know that you stand in contempt of court?"

"You are talk through my hat. I'm stand in door. The sheriff say no man ees to spik weeth these prisoner. Eef you try to pass, *señores*, I mus' weeth moch regret arres' you."

"Well then, arrest me! That's one way of reaching my clients."

Again Joe smiled, almost sadly. "The señor Feesh ees meestake. I'm not lock heem weeth rustlers. No; not beeg good man lak heem. I'm han'cuff heem to the ring in the safe, then even eef the floor she ees saw, the *señor* weel not fall t'rough."

Whereupon both Sylvester Fish and Thaddeus Poole abandoned their legal phraseology, which, by this time, they were convinced was being wasted, and resorted to good old-fashioned cuss words, the intent if not the meaning of which is perfectly understandable to all nationalities. They read Joe's pedigree from the time of Adam to the present, and then into the future for several generations, the while Joe listened with perfect courtesy, even smiling a bit. When they had exhausted their breath, he spoke gently.

"The steam she ees all blow off, eh? Then the *señores* weel oblige by walk somew'ere and jump een reever."

He was no longer smiling, and his eyes were hard; furthermore, the gun in his hand was extended suggestively. The two lawyers, trembling with rage, abruptly turned and stamped down the hall.

Supper time brought a man from the hotel with several pots of food and a basket of utensils. Joe watched while he dished out the nine portions, then assisted in carrying it to the prisoners. When they had finished their meal he helped collect the dishes, and after the hotel man had gone, again searched both prisoners and cells.

The night jailer arrived, and Joe asked the two day men to remain on duty until he had eaten his own supper.

"No one ees to see the prisoners," he told them impressively. "These ees w'at Sheriff Bob say."

"Not even with a court order?" grinned one of the day men who had witnessed the clash between the deputy and the combined legal talent of both prosecution and defense.

Joe eyed him blandly. "May be you no read *Ingles* too, eh?"

"Not a word," the jailer assured him, "except newspapers, magazines, stock journals, reward notices, mail order catalogs, and letters from home."

"You are well educate'," said Joe approvingly, and went to supper.

When he returned it was dark. Instead of going

directly to the jail he circled the courthouse and glanced upward at the barred windows in the rear of the second story. They were inaccessible without the use of a ladder, and even an indifferent jailer would be sure to hear the sound of file or saw on the iron bars. Escape at this point was well nigh impossible.

Joe next visited the corral where twelve captured horses nibbled contentedly at their hay, and the saddle shed with its rack of twelve captured saddles. Some of these bore dark stains on their leather. Satisfied, Joe returned to the jail and dismissed the day men.

For a while he talked with the night jailer, then went into the office. The lamp in the corridor had been lighted, and Joe left the office door open. Placing his gun on a chair by the cot, he stretched out for a nap. About eleven he awoke, and, after visiting the jail, went downstairs and circled the building again. He found nothing to arouse his suspicion, and returned to the office for a bit more of much needed sleep.

Hardly had he entered the building when a dark-clothed figure left the shadows of the adjacent building and walked quickly to the corral. One by one he led horses from the inclosure and saddled them until nine of the animals stood tied to the rails. The moon was shining, but so quietly was the work accomplished that no attention was directed to the space behind the courthouse.

Going to a point directly beneath the second story window nearest the corner of the building, Duke Haslam produced a ball of soft cord. Stepping back a pace or two he looked upward, gauged the distance, and tossed the ball. It struck beneath the sill without a sound and dropped to the ground. He picked it up, threw it again. This time it passed between two of the bars.

Duke quickly moved to the shadows from whence he had emerged and waited. Presently the white ball appeared, unwinding as it fell. Duke stooped, picked up a bag which lay at his feet, and carried it to the corner of the courthouse building.

From the bag he took a Colt revolver and, breaking the cord, tied the end to the trigger guard. A foot above the weapon he tied a short length of wood, then tugged at the line gently and stepped back ino the shadows.

Slowly the gun was drawn upward, occasionally bumping softly against the wall. It reached the sill of the window, disappeared inside. Then the string, weighed by the wood, was let down, and the operation was repeated until four of the sinister weapons were in the hands of the prisoners. When the cord descended again, Duke jerked it and the far end was released. He rolled it into a ball and tossed it to one side, then vanished in the darkness.

Some time later the dozing turnkey was awakened by a low moaning which came from the center cell. He opened his eyes, sat up quickly, and asked, "What's the matter in there?"

His answer was another low groan. Getting to his feet he walked over to one cell and peered through the bars.

"Freeze where you are!" came a low hissed command from the cell to his right. The jailer turned his head. The two inmates were on their knees, a sixgun in the hand of each pointing at him through the bars.

He glanced to his left to find a man in the cell there covering him. When he dazedly looked back at the center cell, the prisoner who had been doing the groaning also held a threatening gun. The jail seemed suddenly to have sprouted lethal weapons.

"Unlock the door, and do it without makin' no noise," came the order.

Reluctantly the jailer did as he was told. He required no one to tell him that these men were desperate and would shoot at the drop of a hat. He unlocked the center door and passed the keys to one of the two men who emerged. Without waste of time they liberated their seven companions, then bound and gagged the jailer and tiptoed from the room.

It was probably the extinguishing of the corridor lamp which awoke Joe, for the escaping prisoners made no sound as they passed along the hall in their stockinged feet. The Mexican's eyes blinked open, and for a moment he lay on the cot staring toward what should have been the lighted quadrangle of the doorway. In that first moment the thought occurred to him that he must be facing the blank wall, to be followed by the realization that if this was so he should be lying on his right side instead of his left.

Joe sat up and orientated himself by the moonlight which showed through the office window. The corridor light, he decided, must have gone out. Ever wary, he buckled on his sixgun and walked out into the hall. Striking a match, he applied the flame to the wick of the lamp which stood on a wall bracket, then turned toward the cell room. Might as well make a round now that he was awake.

He opened the door of the dimly lighted room and stared down at the trussed form of the jailer. Bending over, he tore the gag from the man's mouth. His Latin temperament called for futile oaths and a hearty berating of the unfortunate jailer; but his long association with Bob had taught him tolerance and restraint.

"How eet 'appen?" he asked tersely.

"Got me over to the cell by groanin' like he was sufferin', then four of 'em stuck guns in my face. Four of 'em! I had to let them out. They ain't been gone more than a minute."

Joe did not wait to sever the bonds, but turned and sped along the corridor and down the stairs. He moved swiftly but noiselessly. As he rounded the rear corner of the building he met a file of horsemen who were walking their mounts along the alley. Joe raised his gun and fired.

A man cried out and sagged over the saddle horn. Then a half-dozen guns spoke, and Joe went down. Rolling over on his stomach he fired again. In the moonlight and with such tall targets he could not miss. Again and again he fired, until the gun was empty and a red mist before his eyes obscured the forms of the moving horsemen.

Bullets thudded into the dust about him, snatched at his clothing, seared his arm and leg and side; but he was lying in the shadows and after his five shots were exhausted they had no more flashes at which to shoot. Somebody shouted a command and the survivors broke their horses into a run. One of the riders, bent far over in agony, clung desperately to his saddle horn; the arm of another hung limply. Sprawled on the ground between courthouse and corral were two who would never rustle cows again. And back in the shadows of the building lay José Villegas.

People were stirring now, rushing out of houses half dressed. Somebody found the bound turnkey, who, as soon as he had been freed, led the way to the rear of the building. He sent a man after Doc Witherspoon, then, as the only representative of the law present, formed a posse and set out in pursuit of the escaped prisoners.

The doctor was working over Joe when Bob drove up in the spring wagon. He had stopped at Witherspoon's house and had been directed here by the doctor's wife. Having finished dressing Joe's wounds, the doctor went out to look at Deuce, and Bob knelt by his swarthy but loyal deputy.

"How you makin' it, old-timer?" he asked softly.

Joe looked up at him gravely. "Me, I'm mak out fine," he gasped. "But I am desolate'. The prisoners you lef' in my charge are go. I'm dumb peeg!"

"You're solid gold, Joe. You should have let them go. The whole bunch is not worth yore little finger. I'm proud of you. You got two of them, and I'll bet some more are carryin' yore trademark."

Joe's face lighted up. "Ees good! Me, I'm theenk I'm heet more den pack-'orse dis tam!"

"I'll tell a man! Listen, Joe. The doc is workin' on Deuce. The little fella got Shab Cannon, but Cole Bradshaw shot him up considerable. Deuce is on some mattresses in a spring wagon, and I'm goin' to take him to the Tumblin' T. How'd you like to go along?"

"I'm lak dat fine!"

It was dawn when the spring wagon arrived at the Tumbling T. June prepared beds, and Tomlinson's men carried the two wounded deputies into the house. Bob remained only long enough to snatch a bite to eat, then borrowed a horse from Tomlinson and started back toward Redrock.

Since noon of the preceding day he had been driving the spring wagon at a snail's pace so as not to jolt the wounded Deuce. He had not slept, and the meal he had just eaten was the first since breakfast of the day before. But he could not stop to rest now. Things were approaching a climax. Two of his deputies had been desperately wounded, and he owed it to them and to the office he held to bring justice to those who were responsible.

He had deliberately avoided meeting June, reluctant to confirm her fear about Dick. No longer could he spare Markley and be true to the oath he had taken. As long as he believed there was a chance to win the young man from the company he was keeping he had been lenient to the point of disloyalty to his badge; but Dick had turned his back on the offer which would have meant financial independence and a life of respectability.

Bob rode steadily all morning, and when, half way to Redrock, he saw a rider approaching at a rapid pace, he drew rein and waited for him.

The man pulled up his blowing horse. "You don't happen to be Sheriff Bob Lee, do you?"

"I'm Lee. What is it?"

"I'm one of two boys yore deputy picked up to help chase them holdups. He sent me after you. We got them bottled up in a cabin three miles the other side of Redrock. Come a-humpin'."

Bob felt a tightening about his chest. The showdown with Dick had come.

Chapter XVIII

THE JACK AND THE JOKER

THE cowboy told his story as they rode along the trail. Ace had lost no time in starting after Bradshaw and Markley. With the two cowpunchers whose services he had enlisted, he had picked up the trail and followed it out of Redrock.

"Trail kept to the stage road for a piece, headin' due south; but we knew they would be afraid to ride into Jupiter, because it's a right big town and the end of the stage line. The messenger they'd potted lived there, and they'd 'a' shore got their hides loaded the minute they was recognized. Also they couldn't keep on to the border, for they had no supplies and the country is right rough."

"They circled?"

"They did. We lost the trail and rode back to Redrock. Spelled each other watchin' that crooked exdeputy, and shore enough come evenin' he slipped into the store and bought a lot of grub. We followed him to a basin three miles south-west of town, where he camped. Got as near as we dared and took turns watchin'. That long deputy of yores was on the job when the two rode in early this mornin'. He jumped them, and they broke for a cabin at the foot of the rimrock.

"This Ace fella had no rifle, but he banged away with his sixgun and hit Bradshaw's horse. The critter run a hundred yards before he fell. Ace would 'a' got the jigger, for Bradshaw was stunned, but that Markley fella rode back and pulled him up behind him. By the time we got the horses and started after them they had reached the cabin. They're there now, and unless we get 'em before dark we can kiss 'em good-by."

The reason for this positive statement became apparent to Bob when, shortly afternoon, they joined Ace and the other cowboy. The cabin in which Bradshaw and Dick had taken refuge nestled at the foot of the rimrock. Centuries before, some mighty upheaval had split the barrier, creating a cleft probably a hundred feet wide. Eroded rock and rubble had half filled this immense crack, and across this debris a trail led to the barren, rocky country beyond.

"They cain't cross in the daylight," the cowboy explained, "because that fill is higher than the roof of the cabin and we could pick 'em off with rifles; but when night comes they can sneak over that trail and thumb their noses at us."

"Any way of gettin' in the pass from behind?"

"There ain't a horse livin' that can climb that rimrock, and if you do it afoot it would take days to cut in behind them. The only other way would be to follow the stage road south from Redrock and then cut in behind the hills; but that's awful rough travelin', and I reckon you'd stumble around a long while before findin' that pass. No sir; we get 'em while daylight lasts or we don't get 'em at all."

"We'll have to do our best to hit one of them," Bob decided. "One man cain't defend both ends of the cabin at the same time. Spread out and lie low. Keep pumpin' lead through the windows and the door."

They set about the grim task, stretching out in a thin line and maintaining a slow but steady fire. There was no response from the cabin; the two were quite aware that if they kept whole until nightfall they would be able to slip over the rubble in the cleft and win free.

After an hour or so of this sniping, Bob recalled his men and outlined a simple plan which had occurred to him. They received it doubtfully.

"Too risky for you," Ace summed up their objections. "I'd rather rush them from four different points."

"They could pick us off at their leisure," Bob vetoed shortly. "They're behind shelter, and we cain't run and shoot at the same time. No, this is the only way. Now you two boys remember yore part: work over to the extreme right so you will be shootin' through the windows diagonally. Start pumpin' lead as soon as you get set. Ace, come with me."

Still shaking his head dubiously, the long cowboy followed his chief along the gully and through the chaparral to a point some distance left of the cabin. They moved cautiously in order that their progress would not be detected by Dick and Bradshaw.

"You stay here," Bob told Ace finally. "Get down behind that bush and draw a bead on the near window. Sight just inside the lower right-hand corner. When I make my play, they'll shoot at me from the right of the windows, because it's the only place they'll be safe from the cross fire. If I got it figured right you won't have to find yore target; the target will pop right up in front of yore sights. When it does, don't miss."

"If it's Bradshaw I shore won't," Ace promised grimly.

"Don't bother with the man at the other window. You hold on one until you get him. . . . There goes the boys openin' up. I'll slide over to the left fifty feet or so. Remember, when he takes a shot at me, get him."

Before Ace could object he was gone, worming his way through the brush to the point he had selected.

For several minutes the two cowboys threw hot lead into the cabin, their bullets cutting through the openings diagonally from right to left. Bob, crouching behind his shelter, could see Ace stretched on the ground, rifle stock cuddled against cheek. He picked a clump of rocks some hundred feet ahead as his objective, drew a long breath, and, rising suddenly to his feet, ran in a swift zig-zag course toward them.

His eyes were on the cabin windows, and almost instantly he saw a shadowy form at the far one, caught the glint of the barrel as the rifle was raised. Bob felt a violent tug at his right hip and was thrown off stride. Recovering, he continued toward the rocks. The bullet had struck his holstered gun.

A head appeared at the second window, and eyes which Bob could not see at that distance squinted along the rifle barrel. Bob leaped frantically from side to side, the remorseless muzzle of the weapon following each movement. The rocks were still thirty feet away. It seemed to Bob that, twist and turn as he might, the muzzle of the rifle ever anticipated him. Another shot came from the far window and Bob's hat was snatched from his head. The rocks seemed farther off than ever.

And then, just as he had mentally tensed himself against the impact of a bullet from the near window, Ace's rifle cracked. Bob dived behind the rock cluster and quickly peered over their tops. The head had disappeared within the cabin, and the rifle, after teetering on the sill for a moment, dropped outside.

He heard a wild yell from the far end of the line and turned his head to see the two cowboys sprinting across the open space toward the cabin. The rifle at the second window spoke, and they dropped flat on the ground. Then Ace fired again, driving the unwounded outlaw from his position.

The rest of the fight was of short duration. Advancing alternately, the four reached shelter within sixgun range of the cabin. Under cover of a hail of lead, Bob sprinted around the end of the shack and kicked open the rear door. The firing had ceased the instant he reached the cabin. Dick Markley, crouching in a corner, leveled his gun; then with a savage oath hurled it from him.

"It would have to be you," he said bitterly.

"Is Bradshaw dead?"

Bradshaw himself answered. "I'm goin'—fast. That was—slick work, Lee. Let me—talk to Dick—alone."

"Shore you don't want to talk to me, Brad?"

"I'm no—squealer. It's Dick—I want."

Bob waved back Ace and the cowboys, who were about to enter the rear door. He joined them, and they stood in a sober little knot outside while Dick crossed to his stricken partner and knelt on the floor beside him. They talked in whispers so low that Bob could not hear a word.

"Listen, Dick," Bradshaw was saying. "You—save —yore skin. Tell everything: who had Rutherford killed, who—managed the rustlin' game—what bound Kurt and Duke—together."

"Not on yore life," whispered Dick. "I'm no squealer either."

"You—saved my skin—back there. Do as I say. I— gotta talk—fast." He was silent for a moment, gathering his strength. "Duke Haslam double-crossed you, kid. He never meant to give you that other nine thousand. He said he wanted you to stand between us and Lee; well, he lied! He wanted June Tomlinson. Told Kurt, and Kurt told me. Duke figgered she liked you both. Knowed that if you shot Lee, or if he got you, it would clear the trail for him. He—lives—and we—pay. You—tell—"

Bradshaw went limp at Dick's knees. He was dead.

Markley's face was white with wrath. So Duke Haslam had double-crossed him; never intended to pay him. Wanted June! Dick remembered now how Haslam had looked at the girl when he had thought himself unobserved.

He got to his feet and turned to Bob. "I'll come along quietly. No need for the cuffs."

They spent the night at Redrock and started back for Lariat the next morning. Cole Bradshaw was buried near the cabin where he had fallen.

Their arrival at Lariat caused quite a stir. Both Enright and Trumbauer were in town, and both were high in their praise. Kurt Dodd gone; Pete Grubb gone; Shab Cannon gone; Cole Bradshaw gone; Dick Markley in jail. And to crown the thing, the escaped prisoners had been overtaken and captured.

"Py golly! Dot iss vat you call der clean-up, ain't it?" enthused Dutch.

"Not quite," Bob told them soberly. "The big shot is still at large."

"Der pig shot?"

"Duke Haslam. He was behind all this. I know it, but I cain't prove it."

"Ach! Now you chump at gonglusions!"

"I'm not jumpin' at anything. Duke caused Rutherford's death; Duke was behind all this stealin' and killin'. I know it."

"Bob, you must be wrong," Enright protested. "I know you hate the jigger and so do I; but—why, that strong box on the stage had Duke's money in it. He wouldn't steal his own gold."

"Of course he would. He wouldn't be losing anything. Listen, Frank. Somebody tossed a ball of cord into the jail and sent up four guns. Somebody saddled nine horses. The only ones of the gang left were Shab, Cole, and Dick. They were in Redrock. Who was in Lariat to do it?"

"Mebbe one of the gang you failed to get; or a friend."

"Well, we won't argue. I tried to get Bradshaw to talk, but he wouldn't. Just remember what I told you. Where is Duke?"

"Out at the Kady. He holds a mortgage on it, and moved over there to take stock. A crew of six rode in yesterday, now that the old outfit's gone."

"Und, py golly! dey vas tough looking fellas, too!"

"That's the kind he uses. . . . Here he comes now!"

Duke Haslam, resplendent in range clothing, rode a beautiful bay to the hitching rack and dismounted. To Bob's surprise he came directly toward them, hand extended.

"Good work, Lee," he said heartily, overlooking the fact that Bob had failed to notice his hand. "When you took office I had my doubts of you; but you certainly have made good. Markley is the last of them, I understand."

"Not the last, Duke. There is one more."

"Yes? Well, you'll probably land him in time. I'm over at the Kady. Kurt left things in awful shape. Never knew how lax he was, or I wouldn't have lent him money on the spread. I'll see you gentlemen again. When you find time, Bob, ride out to visit me." He smiled and turned into the courthouse. Later, when Bob went into his own office, he saw Haslam in close consultation with Thaddeus Poole and Judge Bleek.

That afternoon Dick was taken before the latter, pleaded not guilty, and was advised that his trial would be held two days hence.

Bob was surprised at the haste, and told Dick so on the way back to the cell room. Dick did not appear to be worried. He was tight-lipped and grim. "The sooner the better," he said. "I'll serve my time, and when I get out I'll have a debt to pay."

"Dick, I reckon you know what it cost me to do this."

Markley's face softened. "Lord love you, Bob, I

wasn't thinkin' of you. It's Duke Haslam. He double-crossed me."

Bob spoke eagerly. "I accepted the nomination just to get the goods on that jigger! Dick, tell the truth about him, and I'll guarantee you a pardon."

Dick shook his head. "Bradshaw told me about Haslam, and wanted me to talk. But I'm no squealer. I'll pay my own debts."

Bob could not move him; Dick would not be swayed. "I'll do what I can for you anyhow, Dick. I know you were led into this, and I'll make it a point to tell the Governor so when I ask for yore pardon. Keep yore chin up, son."

Dick tried to speak, choked, blinked his eyes, and turned into the cell.

"Would you like to see—anybody?" Bob asked hesitatingly.

Dick shook his head. "No."

Much as Bob wished to visit Deuce and Joe, he did not go to the Tumbling T; and once, when he saw June ride into town, he ducked into his office and locked the door. He did not want to see her; the thought of what she must be suffering cut him to the quick. He could not face her, for while he had done the only thing possible in capturing Dick, he realized that if she loved the boy she would always feel bitter toward the one who had apprehended him. She would not realize that this thing his duty had forced upon him had caused him as much agony as it could have brought to her. Man's love for man goes deep.

From Ace he learned that both Deuce and the Mexican were getting along as well as could be expected. June was in almost constant attendance, and to her skill and devotion they owed much of their steady improvement.

The trial attracted comparatively little attention. The rustling ring had been broken up, Grubb, Dodd, Cannon, and Bradshaw were dead, the case against Markley was a cut and dried one. Haslam was there, and beside him sat June Tomlinson. Bob carefully avoided meeting her glance. Watching surreptitiously he noticed that her face was drawn and that there were shadows under the violet eyes.

The charges against Dick were highway robbery and murder; but since the actual killer of the messenger had been identified as Cole Bradshaw, it was the general opinion that Dick would receive a jail sentence under the robbery charge. And if Haslam's prosecuting attorney ran true to form the jail sentence would probably be light.

Great was the surprise when Thaddeus Poole reverted to the remorseless prosecutor he was at one time reputed to be. He paraded before the court, he thundered at the jury, he gouged Dick unmercifully, picturing him as a second Billy the Kid, the associate of killers, a potential murderer himself. Toward the end of his summing up speech, Bob's apprehensions rose, and he suddenly realized that for once practically every member of the jury was a rabid Clean-up Party man. To add to his worry, Sylvester Fish's defense of Dick was lukewarm and half-hearted, and Judge Bleek was suffering from one of his "spells."

The jury found a verdict of guilty on both counts, and Judge Bleek sentenced Dick to death by hanging, said hanging to be performed by the sheriff on the morning of the following Friday.

For a moment the severity of the sentence left the spectators stunned; then as Bleek rose to leave the bench, a loud murmur swept through the courtroom. Savage satisfaction, hearty approval, a few regrets that such harsh punishment had been meted out. Bob gazed dumbly at the prisoner. Dick was staring out into the audience, and Bob had never before seen such concentrated hate in a man's eyes.

He followed the direction of Dick's gaze and found himself looking at Duke Haslam. At the moment Haslam was unaware of their scrutiny. One arm was about the shoulders of June Tomlinson, who, with lowered head, was crying. A mighty rage welled up within Bob and for a moment his face was a mirror of Dick's.

Leaving Markley under the watchful eye of Ace, he strode swiftly to the rear door, through which Judge Bleek was about to pass. Roughly he gripped the man by a shoulder and swung him about.

Bleek's eyes flashed angrily. "What do you mean by this, Lee? I'm no sack of salt to be pushed about this way."

"I don't know what you are," said Bob hotly. "You shore ain't a man, to let yore petty infirmities warp yore sense of justice. You've condemned to death a kid who was led by older, more vicious companions, and you've satisfied yore personal spite by orderin' me, his best friend, to hang him. Well, that's one thing you or nobody else can make me do! Here are my badge and keys. I'm through—done—resigned! If you want it in writin' you shore can have it."

He flung the badge and keys on the floor at Bleek's feet, and, pushing the man roughly aside, walked blindly through the rear doorway.

Chapter XIX

THURSDAY NIGHT

B OB LEE sat at a table in the Paris saloon frowning at the glass before him. Opposite him sat Ace, staring just as moodily at the face of his friend. It had occurred to Ace with something of a shock that Bob had aged these last few days. His shoulders drooped, the eyes were somber and brooding, cheek and forehead lines were deeper.

Ace stirred restlessly. "Dang it! If Dick would only talk."

Bob answered gloomily. "It's my failure to hear from the Governor that worries me. I wired him; sent the telegram on the stage two days ago. I told him I was resignin' as sheriff because I couldn't bring myself to hang a boy who was sentenced by a prejudiced judge. I asked for a postponement. This is Thursday afternoon. I cain't get a reply now until tomorrow mornin's stage gets in, and that will be too late."

"I don't see how come Bleek to hand out that sentence. I always thought he was part of the Haslam machine."

"He is. That's why he sentenced Dick to death." Then, as Ace looked puzzled, he went on to explain. "Dick is the only one alive who can testify to Duke's connection with Kurt Dodd and the rest. Kurt shot

Pete Grubb to prevent his talkin'; Duke Haslam would hang Dick for the same purpose."

"Good, gallopin' grandmas! And Dick refuses to talk."

"He expected a jail sentence. Even now he'll be expectin' Duke to get him out some way."

"Damn Duke Haslam anyway!" swore Ace throatily. "He's behind the whole works and we cain't pin a thing on him. And Miss June a-cryin'—" He broke off. "Shucks; I would go and say that."

"You didn't tell me anything I haven't guessed. That's the tough part. She loves Dick. With him it's a quick drop and the end; but she has to go through the years—"

"Yeah, I know." Ace assumed an optimism he did not feel. "Mebbe that message will come through in time after all." He got to his feet. "I'm goin' to look up Frank Enright. See you later."

Bob sat frowning at the glass for some minutes after Ace had gone. Tomorrow morning Dick would hang. The resignation of the sheriff would not stay the execution; Haslam wanted Dick hanged, and would have Bleek appoint some one to do the job. And Haslam would sit out at the Kady smiling complaisantly and puffing on a fat cigar, when he should be the one standing on the trap with the sinister knot behind his ear.

Bob looked up suddenly, aware that save for himself the room was empty. The bartender had stepped outside to speak to a friend. Bob got to his feet and crossed the room to the door which opened into Haslam's office. It was unlocked. Bob entered, closed the

door behind him, and shot the bolt. Crossing swiftly
to the one which opened into the dining room, he tried
it. Locked. To be sure, he drew the bolt, then went to
the desk and seated himself before it. One by one he
pulled out the drawers and looked over their contents.
He found account books and records covering the operation of hotel and saloon, canceled checks, stationery,
odds and ends.

The pidgeon holes before him contained trifles:
scratch pads, pencils, pens, erasers. A cigar box occupied one of the larger compartments. Bob removed it
in order to look behind it, noticed a bit of letter paper
projecting from beneath the lid, opened it. Not cigars,
but papers. He went through them quickly. Nothing he
wanted. And then, at the very bottom, a picture.

He took it up and studied it. Two young men, standing side by side, one of them Duke Haslam of perhaps
a decade before. The face of the other was vaguely
familiar. Bob turned over the photograph, read the
inscription on the back, then swore in amazement.
Thrusting the picture into a pocket, he finished his
search, then quietly unbolted both doors and left by
means of the window.

Circling the building, he entered the saloon. Several
men were at the bar, talking. One of them was Ace,
and at sight of Bob the tall cowboy hastened to join
him. His face was tight, his eyes glinted with excitement.

"You heard the news? Bleek just appointed Duke
Haslam actin' sheriff!"

"Haslam!"

"Yeah. The danged double-crossin' rattler!"

Bob told Ace he'd see him later, and went out of the
Paris. This was the last straw. Duke Haslam, the
biggest rascal of them all, parading as sheriff of the
county! Duke Haslam hanging a man who had served
him loyally, and who, but for him, would this day have
been a respected member of the community instead of
a convicted thief and potential killer!

Bob went into the hotel and bought a sheet of paper
and an envelope. At a desk in the corner he penned a
short note, which, together with the photograph, he
sealed within the envelope. By the time he had finished
the supper gong had sounded and men were trooping
into the dining room.

Bob joined Ace at the table, and when the meal was
over led the tall cowboy into the lobby and found
chairs. "Charley," he said, "we've been partners for a
long while. Maybe what I'm goin' to do won't stack up
with what you think is right. If so, just holler. I want
you to ride to the Tumblin' T and tell Miss June to
have a saddled horse waitin' at the point where the
trail to her father's spread joins the one to the Kady.
Make it ten o'clock tonight."

"That ain't askin' so much. But why Miss June?
I can bring the horse there myself."

"I want her to be there. I think she'd like to. Somebody might have a message for her. If you'd like to
ride with her—well, I'd be a heap obliged."

Ace nodded soberly. "Shore I'll ride with her. But
mebbe I'd better come back after deliverin' yore message. You might—uh—get lonely, or need help, or
somethin'."

"I'll be all right; you stay with her. And, Ace," he

fished the envelope from his pocket, "I wish you'd keep this until mornin'. If I'm not at the Tumblin' T by daylight, open it and read what's inside, then lay the whole thing before Frank Enright and tell him to go to the Governor with it."

Ace accepted the envelope and put it in his pocket. "I shore wish you'd take me in on this, Bob."

Bob smiled. "You can help best by doin' just as I say. You'd better start now."

They got up, and for a long moment looked into each other's eyes. "Be seein' you," said Ace, and reluctantly turned away.

Bob waited until he heard the drum of hoofs which told of Ace's departure, then went into the saloon and sat down at a corner table. An hour passed. Men came in and went out again, but Duke Haslam was not among them. Bob waited another hour or so, then got up and sauntered from the place.

For several minutes he stood on the sidewalk, smoking. Presently he ground the cigarette butt beneath his heel and walked swiftly along the passage at the side of the building to the alley behind. At the building adjoining the courthouse he halted. There was a light in the jail section, and another farther forward, near the head of the stairs. That would be Poole's office.

Bob gazed thoughtfuly at the jail light. No chance to duplicate Duke Haslam's trick with the ball of cord, for Dick occupied a cell without a window. Only one thing to do: walk in there and take him out by force.

Bob made his way to the corral, caught Dick's horse and saddled him, leaving the animal tied beneath the shed. Making his way along the side of the building, he waited at the corner until he was certain there was no one near to observe him, then removed his spurs and slipped quietly up the steps to the portico and entered the open front doorway.

At one side of the corridor and directly ahead of him were the stairs. He mounted them silently, mentally condemning the upstairs hall light which made his movements plain to anybody who happened to be passing. The building was inordinately silent.

At the top of the flight he paused, listening. A short distance ahead and to his right was the open doorway to Poole's office. He heard a dry cough. Judge Bleek. Bob tiptoed to the far side of the corridor, inched along the wall. He could see, diagonally through the doorway, the back of a chair and part of the body in it. A foot farther. The occupant was Judge Bleek. He was studying the board before him. Bob inched forward another foot—two. The bloated features of Thaddeus Poole came into view. He, too, was intent on the game of chess. The judge reached out a skinny hand, moved a piece, chuckled drily as he captured one of Poole's bishops. Poole uttered a fervent "Damn!" and Bob leaped as lightly as a shadow across the bar of light from the room.

He wheeled, gun in hand, listening. The two were talking; he had not been seen. Crossing the corridor he turned down the wick of the wall bracket lamp. The flame sputtered and went out. Ahead of him was the door to the cell room, closed.

Bob reached it, grasped the knob, turned. The door was locked. Undecided, he stood there debating his next move. From down the hall came a guffaw of glee as Poole engineered a coup against his opponent. The judge's voice rose in protest, and under cover of the sound Bob rapped sharply on the panel.

The door opened a crack and a gun barrel was thrust through. Above it appeared the suspicious face of the night jailer. Bob reached out swiftly, grasping the gun so that his left thumb was wedged between cocked hammer and chamber. He felt the firing pin pierce his flesh as the fellow squeezed the trigger. Pushing against the door with his whole weight, Bob leaped after the surprised jailer and brought the barrel of his Colt down on the fellow's bare head. As the man wilted he caught him and eased him to the floor. Quickly he closed the door and bolted it.

He heard Dick's surprised voice. "Bob! What are you doin'?"

Lee found the keys and unlocked the cell door. Dick stepped out. Again he asked, "Bob, what are you doin'?"

Bob turned to him. "Not so loud. If those boots squeak, take them off. We've got to get past Poole's door. Take the jailer's gun. Yore horse is saddled and waitin' under the shed. Get on him and fork it along the Kady trail. June is waitin' at the branch leadin' to the Tumblin' T with a fresh mount. Take it and head for the Bottle Neck. Keep on until you're across the border. Come on."

As silently as two shadows they stole along the corridor. They had reached a point some ten feet from the lighted doorway of Poole's office when they heard the scrape of a chair.

"That lamp's gone out," came Poole's heavy voice.

"I'll have to light it. Some of Markley's friends might try a jail delivery."

"Friends?" came Bleek's sour voice. "Didn't know he had any, except our ex-sheriff, and he's too honest to try a trick like that." There was a sneer in Bleek's tones. "Upright member of the Cleanup Party, you know."

Bob pushed Dick before him and motioned to the stairs. Dick stood stubbornly where he was. Again Bob gestured, and risked a fierce whisper.

"For God's sake go! I'll take care of them."

The whispered answer came back to him, equally fierce. "No, by God!"

Then Thaddeus Poole stepped into the corridor.

Bob leaped forward and his left fist came up in an arc which landed exactly on the point of Poole's jaw. The man went over backwards and landed like a wet dishrag on the office floor. Leaping after him, Bob leveled his gun at the astonished Bleek. The judge had half risen from his chair, his hands on the edge of the table before him.

"Keep them there!" snapped Bob. "And don't let out a single yap. I'm honin' to settle yore hash, Bleek; just you give me the chance!"

"Why, you—"

"Shut up!" Bob thrust his gun into its holster and, leaping forward, grasped the man by the throat and forced him back into the chair. Circling his neck with a strong arm, Bob pulled a handkerchief from his pocket and stuffed it into Bleek's mouth; binding it in place with his neckerchief. Raising the skinny man from the chair, Bob threw him, rolled him on his face and, despite his desperate struggles, tied his hands behind him with his own necktie. It was a crude job, but the tie was strong and the knot tight.

Dick was standing in the doorway. "Get out of here," Bob commanded curtly. "You can't help me one bit."

"Not without you."

"I'll follow in a minute. If anybody comes in here you won't stand a chance. You're simply endangerin' both of us by stayin'."

The argument was effective; Dick turned toward the stairs.

Bob found some heavy twine in a desk drawer and made a more thorough job of it, binding and gagging both men securely. Then, dousing the light and locking the door behind him, he made his way to the street. Ducking back to the alley, he heard the faint drum of hoofs in the distance. Dick had gone.

Bob walked swiftly to the Paris and looked over the half doors of the saloon. Duke Haslam was not in sight. He nodded grimly and turned to his horse. Duke was at the Kady. Well, now that he had started he might as well see the thing through. *He* knew Haslam was guilty, and if there was a God in Heaven, He knew it too. Somehow he'd force his way into Duke Haslam's presence, brand him for what he was, slap his face, dare him to draw. Then if it pleased that same God, he'd down this maker of murderers and follow Dick to the border. If not—well, Ace and Frank Enright would see that Haslam got his just deserts.

He swung into the saddle and reined away from the rack. Once out of town he put his horse to a steady lope along the trail over which Dick had already sped.

When he neared the junction of the Kady and Tumbling T trails, he angled off to the right, circling at such a distance that June and Ace, if they were still there, would not hear the hoofbeats. Presently he cut into the Kady trail once more and put his horse to a sharper gait.

June and Ace were still there. They had been there since long before the appointed hour. June had listened to Ace's terse message, face pinched, violet eyes wide.

"Of course I'll do it," she said. "Oh, Ace, what is it all coming to?"

"I don't know. Dang it all, Bob just couldn't stand seein' you suffer the rest of yore days. Neither could I. Miss June, he'd turn Duke Haslam himself loose if it would make you happy."

"He'd do that—for me?" she faltered.

"Yes'm. I been watchin' Bob a long while. Reckon he loves you, ma'am. That's why he's freein' Dick. He knows it would break yore heart to—to have them do what they figgered on doin' to him."

"But, Ace, it isn't Dick I care for! Are you blind too? It's—it's Bob!"

Ace stared at her. "Bob! You—you love *Bob!* Oh, my gosh!"

They waited at the intersection of the trails for more than an hour before the drum of hoofs notified them of the approach of a horseman. They were standing in the shadows, but as the horseman drew up Ace stepped into the moonlight.

"Who is it?" came Dick's voice.

"Me—Ace. Miss June has a horse for you. Where's Bob?"

Dick swung from the saddle. "He said he'd be right behind me. Where's June?"

"Back there by them trees. I'll change yore rig for you." Ace took the horse in charge, leaving Dick to make his way to the girl.

"Dick," said June quietly, "Bob saved you again, probably at the risk of his own liberty if not his life. He did it because of his love for you, and because he believes that I care for you."

Dick groaned. "I wish to God you did! I tell you, it's drivin' me mad! I think of you every—"

"Hush!" she admonished softly. "It's so useless, Dick. From the first I have cared for Bob. Ace just told me that Bob loves me. Neither of us has ever mentioned the subject; and now perhaps he will never know."

Dick could see the misery in her eyes. "I want to think this out," he told her hoarsely. For a long while he paced up and down, hands locked behind him, chin on breast.

Ace came up, leading the fresh horse. "If Bob was comin' he'd be here by now. You better not wait, Dick. If they've caught Bob they'll be after you, and you need all the start you can get. You fork it away from here."

Dick looked up then, and in the moonlight they saw that his face was set in hard, determined lines. "You're right. So long, both of you." He sprang into the saddle and spurred away.

June and Ace sat down on a rock and waited for another five minutes. Ace was restless.

"Dang it!" he exclaimed at last. "This waitin' gets

me. June, Bob gave me a letter to be opened in the mornin' if he didn't show up. I may be doin' wrong, but I'm goin' to open it now." When she nodded approval he produced the envelope and ripped open the flap.

"We'll need some light for this," he said, and, gathering some dry brush, started a little fire. Heads together they studied the picture, then read the carefully written note. It detailed the various circumstances whereby Bob was convinced that Duke Haslam was the prime mover behind Dodd's gang, including the conversation with Dick. From there on the letter read as follows:

The enclosed picture is another and final link in the chain. It shows two men, brothers according to the inscription on the back. One is Duke Haslam; the other Kurt Dodd Haslam. Using only his first two names, the latter established himself near Lariat and undoubtedly worked hand in glove with his brother, Duke supplying the brainwork, Kurt the physical force necessary in bank and payroll robberies, cattle theft, and murders.

By the time you read this, the issue will be definitely settled. Where the law has failed I trust I shall not. I intend to force my way into Haslam's presence and settle the thing man to man. If I do not return, I ask that this photograph and letter be placed in the hands of the Governor.

Robert Lee.

Ace swore. "He's goin' out there to face Haslam! And Duke with six bad *hombres* to protect him! June, wait here in case he comes along. If he does, for gosh sake hold him. I'll get yore father's crew and come a-runnin'." He was gone before she could utter a word.

June stood listening until the drumming hoofbeats died in the distance. Despite the furious pounding of her heart, the blood had drained from her face. Something told her that Bob had already passed; that her waiting here was in vain.

With a little desperate cry she turned, sprang into the saddle, and, wheeling her pony into the trail, set him at a thundering gallop toward the Kady.

CHAPTER XX

PAID IN LEAD

WHILE still a mile from the Kady buildings Bob dismounted and led his horse. When at last he rounded the corrals, it was to see a dim light in the bunkhouse and another shining through the windows of the ranch house parlor.

Tying the reins loosely to a rail, Bob stood searching the shadows about the house for a full five minutes, then hitched his gun belt and strode quickly across the moonlit space. Silently mounting the steps he traversed the gallery and slipped through the open doorway into the room. Immediately he stepped one pace to the left, putting the wall at his back.

Haslam was seated at a table, a lighted lamp at his elbow. Before him were spread books and papers which he appeared to be studying. Bob considered him steadily: the smooth black hair, thinning at the top; the heavy jowls; the sensuous lips, curled as ever around a cigar; the short thick hands, well-kept and soft. Bob thought of a plump, lazy grub; a blood-sucking, flesh-consuming grub.

Perhaps it was the intensity of his stare which caught Haslam's attention. He looked up suddenly and Bob saw his face contort in a tiny spasm, his eyes widen, then go narrow. The hand which gripped a pen tensed, relaxed.

"You invited me over to see you," said Bob softly. "I'm here."

"What do you want? Nothing important, is it? I'm right busy now."

"You'll be busier in a minute. Duke, I've done my best to pin the deadwood on you in such a way that the law would handle you as you deserve. I couldn't do it. I know you're a liar, a thief, a murderer at heart. I have the proof, but not the kind that a court will consider. So I'm here to try you myself, and I'm actin' as judge, jury, prosecutin' attorney, and executioner all in one."

"You must be crazy," Haslam told him coldly enough; but there was a hint of panic in his eyes.

"You know I'm speakin' the truth. You caused Rutherford to be murdered in the hope of beatin' the Cleanup Party. One of Shab Cannon's men did it, and Shab worked for Kurt Dodd. Kurt, Duke, was yore brother."

Haslam's eyes went wide again, this time in surprise. Bob went on:

"I found that photograph in yore desk. It told me a lot. It told me that the two of you were workin' together to rob the community, you through yore political influence, Kurt through his gang of thieves and killers. Deuce killed Shab, Ace killed Bradshaw, and I killed Dodd. The only one left to connect you with the outfit is Dick. Bradshaw told Dick you double-crossed him, and urged him to talk; but in spite of that Dick kept quiet. So you escaped the law again. This time, Duke, you're not goin' to escape."

Haslam caught the slightest of movements in the darkness outside, but his features did not betray the fact. He knew now that he was safe, that he had not posted guards in vain, and with that knowledge came returned courage and a sudden berserk rage that burst forth like water from a ruined dam.

He got to his feet, keeping his hands on the table. "You're right," he snarled. "I did have Rutherford put away! I did back Kurt and the boys. I've managed holdups, robberies, and killings, and I'll manage them again! But you were wrong when you said Dick is the only one remaining who knows. *You* know; but like Dick you will never use that knowledge. Kurt was my brother, and you killed him. I told you the day you brought his dead body to Lariat that I would get you for that if it was the last thing I did. Well, I'm keeping my word. *Take him, boys!*"

Bob glimpsed the arm which projected itself through the doorway, felt the stab of a gun barrel in his ribs. He pivoted on his right heel, brushing the barrel of the gun toward the wall as he did so. The weapon exploded, but the bullet did not even touch him. Grasping the extended arm, he jerked its owner clear into the room, smashed him on the jaw with a sweeping left that sent him crashing into the far side of the door frame.

Instantly he whirled again to face Haslam, snatched the gun from its holster and flung a hasty shot at Duke; but the owner of the Paris had ducked beneath the table, and the slug did no more than shower him with splinters.

Bob wheeled as another man came running through the doorway, almost colliding with him. Instinctively their arms went about each other, and they staggered across the floor, each attempting to get his gun to bear and at the same time avoid being shot himself.

Boots pounded the veranda floor, confused yells came from the direction of the bunkhouse. They fell over a chair, broke it to fragments, crashed to the floor. Gripping the fellow's gun wrist, Bob pushed himself to his knees and flung another shot toward the table which protected Haslam.

A heavy body struck him from behind, and a muscular arm went about his neck and tightened. Bob staggered to his feet, bent swiftly, and catapulted the attacker clear over his head. The fellow struck a book case and collapsed in a shower of glass. Another grabbed Bob from behind—a fourth. Haslam was shouting, "Shoot the son!" Somebody replied, pantingly, "Careful! You'll hit one of us!"

Bob felt his gun arm seized and cruelly twisted. Involuntarily his fingers released their grip and the weapon thudded to the floor. He shook himself desperately, and by sheer physical force staggered across the floor dragging them with him. His eyes were on the contorted face of Duke Haslam peering over the table top. If only he could live until he had his fingers around that soft throat!

Two more men joined the fray, and Bob was dragged away from the table. Fists thudded into his face, his feet were swept from beneath him by a tangle of human legs. He fell to his knees. A man yelled, "Now! Sock him!" A gun barrel struck him a glancing blow on the head and he fell face down on the floor.

The period of unconsciousness was short. When he opened his eyes he was still on the floor and somebody was kicking him in the side.

"Get up, damn you!" came the frenzied voice of Duke Haslam. "Get up and take it like a man!"

Bob rolled over weakly. Instantly rough hands seized him and he was jerked to his feet. He stood there, giddy and swaying, while they held him.

"Stand him against the wall!" cried Haslam, and Bob was half-pushed, half-carried to one side of the big stone fireplace. They spun him about and thrust his shoulders against the wall, then drew off leaving him to find his balance and support himself by palms pressed flat against the rough plaster.

Haslam was walking back and forth, his fists clenching and unclenching at his sides. The cigar was gone, and his lips were pressed tightly together. He looked and acted like a crazy man.

"By jacks, Bob Lee, you've raised hell for the last time! I swore I'd get you, and I've got you now! Your back's to the wall, right where I want it. I'll show you who's judge, jury, and executioner! Pass me that shotgun."

Bob glanced about him. There didn't seem to be a chance in the world for him. Haslam was mad; utterly mad. The six men were scattered about the room, each with a gun in his hand. Their faces were hard, merciless, drawn in savage anticipation. One of them handed Duke a shotgun.

On the floor a dozen feet away lay Bob's Colt. It had fallen under the shattered remains of the chair. It might just as well have been left in Lariat; they could hit him ten times before he could reach it.

Haslam was standing in the middle of the room, the shotgun gripped tightly in his hands. The light from the lamp shone full on his face; his features were distorted with rage and excitement, his eyes glittered, his hands shook so that the muzzle of the gun wobbled jerkily.

Bob found himself thinking of June. It didn't matter so much about him; without her life would be rather stale at the best. But with Duke Haslam alive she would never be safe. He tensed himself, called upon every bit of reserve strength within him. When Duke started to raise the gun he would dive for the Colt on the floor. They'd get him, of course; all he asked of the Big Judge was that he be allowed to fire one shot into Duke Haslam's soft stomach before he checked out.

"Judge, jury, and executioner!" Haslam was shrilling. "That's me! A one-man firing squad. And in the morning your friend, Dick Markley, will kick holes in the atmosphere."

The hammer of the shotgun clicked as Haslam drew it back to full cock. He started to raise the weapon. Bob gathered himself for the leap.

"Hold it, you double-crossin' polecat!"

The words brought every one of them up with a jolt. Bob saw Haslam jerk as though a bullet had struck him. Gun hands and bodies froze while heads turned slowly, cautiously, toward the source of the sound.

Bob glanced over Haslam's shoulder. Standing in

the doorway which led to the dining room was Dick Markley.

It was a Dick that Bob had never seen before, unless it was that day in the courtroom. He was crouched, cocked gun extended before him, face twisted into a mask of hate. Even while they stared he spoke, his voice low, tense, the words dripping with venom.

"You yellow dog! You'll hang nobody in the mornin'. I'm sendin' you where you belong on a one-way ticket, and I'm sendin' you there tonight!"

The gun flicked upward, steadied; the hammer fell. A futile click!

Instantly Hades broke loose. Duke Haslam wheeled and the shotgun bellowed. Bob dove for the gun on the floor, snatched it up, started shooting. Dick had instantly drawn back the hammer again, and this time the gun did not misfire; but in the meanwhile the six had gotten into action, and Bob saw the boy stagger under the lead which was flung into him. Haslam was down; whether or not he had been hit, Bob did not know.

He himself was kneeling on the floor, shooting under the billowing clouds of smoke. There were but three loaded cartridges in his gun, possibly four in Dick's. And there were seven men facing them, including Haslam. The whole thing was over in the space it would take a man to count five; a sudden, tremendous holocaust like the explosion of a powder magazine, then silence, dreadful, appalling.

Bob was hit three times, but except for the numbing shock of the bullets he was unaware of it. He threw down and aimed carefully before each shot, and every time one of Haslam's men fell. A brief glimpse he had of Dick swaying in the doorway, holding to the jamb to keep his feet, eyes slitted, teeth bared, the gun in his hand spewing flame and lead. Suddenly he saw the boy reel, fall heavily. His own gun hammer fell on an empty, and he realized that there were no more targets at which to shoot. He tried to get to his feet, but his head was buzzing and the swirling powder smoke choked him. He had the crazy impression that he could hear hoofbeats. He fell forward, breaking the fall somewhat with arms from which the strength had gone. Felt good to be lying there. . . . Sleepy . . . awfully . . . sleepy. . . .

Consciousness returned slowly. As though from a great distance he heard a voice—June's voice. Funny. He lay there listening. The voice grew louder; there was a frightened note in its timbre. Then a man spoke. Duke Haslam!

Bob fought upward through the haze. It required the greatest of effort to open his eyes. The room swam about him dizzily, then steadied. In the front doorway stood June Tomlinson, her little thirty-two-twenty extended. Before her was Duke Haslam.

"I tell you to put that gun down and let me out!" snarled Haslam.

"No! If you come a step nearer I'll shoot! I swear I will!"

Haslam leaped forward, landed on the balls of his feet, sprang quickly to his right. The little gun barked —missed. Duke leaped again and his clutching left hand caught the barrel of the gun. The girl whimpered with pain as the weapon was wrenched from her hand.

"You damned little wildcat! Now maybe you'll let me go!"

Like the animal he had called her, she sprang at him. She kicked, she scratched, she drummed a small fist against his heavy face. Duke staggered backwards, hastily threw the gun from him, and seized her. She fought him with the courage of despair, clinging to him, biting the hand which would have throttled her.

Bob pushed himself to his knees, started propelling himself across the floor. His destination was the gun which was clutched in the hand of a dead outlaw. Every forward inch was agony; his arms buckled beneath him, he swayed on all fours like a drunken quadruped.

He reached the gun, took it from the lax fingers which held it. The one arm on which he was supporting himself gave way, and he sprawled on his face. Gathering his strength, he raised the weapon. Curse it! Why couldn't he hold the thing steady!

He noticed now that another figure was moving on the far side of the room. The fellow was dragging himself over the floor, making for the girl's gun which Haslam had tossed to one side. Bob removed his gaze, concentrated on the task before him. His voice came in a hoarse croak.

"Haslam! Hands—off—her!"

Even in that tense moment he heard June's joyous "Bob! Oh, Bob!"

Duke froze, pushed the girl from him as one would rid oneself of a clawing cat. He spun on the balls of his feet, a hand flashing to the hideout holster beneath his left arm. Bob was holding his gun with both hands, two thumbs on the hammer. He saw the flash of Haslam's short-barreled weapon, drew the hammer back—

A shot rang out on the far side of the room, and Duke Haslam brought up with a start as though something had surprised him. He had not yet leveled his weapon. He never did. For a moment he stood there, his mouth working as if he were trying to speak, then he turned, and as he did, the gun barked again. Duke reeled, stumbled forward a pace or two, then crashed to the floor.

Bob turned his eyes toward the man who had fired the shots. It was Dick Markley. He had struggled to his knees, and Bob saw that he was literally shot to pieces. He was staring toward the doorway, where June leaned weakly against the wall. And as he gazed, the harsh lines on his face slowly vanished, the hot blazing eyes softened, the grim lips curved in a smile that was infinitely tender. His voice came to Bob, panting, hesitant, but with a sort of wistful pride in it.

"June—girl! I—made good—after all—didn't I?"

Bob saw her run to him, put her arms about him. But Dick's head had sagged forward, and he was an inert weight in her arms.

And then Bob collapsed too.

Chapter XXI

JOSÉ VILLEGAS SINGS

O NCE more Bob awoke to find himself staring at the rafters of a Tumbling T bedroom. It was evening, and a soft breeze swept through the open window. In an adjoining room a guitar was twanging, and a musical voice hummed a Spanish love song. Bob experienced a little thrill when he identified the voice as belonging to Joe Villegas.

"Hey, you black-eyed son of sin, cut that out! You'll waken Bob."

Another thrill. That was Deuce speaking.

"Ees tam she wake up," came the calm answer. "She ees slip all day."

"Yeah?" came Ace's drawl. "And who's got a better right to sleep? You two dudes been doin' nothin' but eat and sleep while him and me has been cleanin' house."

"Him and who?" inquired Deuce. "Why if they'd 'a' waited for you to get there the whole outfit would 'a' died of old age instead of lead poisonin'."

"Well, I done the best I could. I hadda ride back to see if Miss June had stopped Bob; it wasn't my fault we got there after the party was over."

"Huh! You're just jealous because you didn't stop no lead so's Miss June could take care of you."

"Who's jealous? Me? Why, you bandy-laiged li'l' rooster! When you get well, I'll—"

"No need to wait, you annimated clothes-tree! I'll climb outa this bed and give you a good workin' over right now!"

"*Señores!*" begged Joe. "Wait one moment, plis. I'm jus' theenk of song Mees June ees sing. Eet ees, 'Lock' Een the Stable Weeth the Ship!'"

Deuce guffawed. "Oh, my gosh! Locked in the stable with the sheep! That's 'Rocked in the Cradle of the Deep,' you pore lunkhead."

"Ees no difference; ees same moosic."

"Oh, no; no difference. I reckon 'When the Swaller Homeward Flies' is 'When We Swaller Homemade Pies' to you."

Bob chuckled aloud, heard a little stir beside him.

"Bob!"

A cool little hand found his, clutched it tightly. He turned his head.

"Oh, hello, Miss June. Reckon I'm here to bother you some more."

"Bob, don't say that! We're—all—so glad you are here."

"It's nice of you to say that."

"Bob, listen. A wire came from the Governor this morning. He refuses to accept your resignation!"

He eyed her soberly. "And Dick?"

"Dick is—dead. He died in my arms, smiling. Oh, Bob, wasn't he noble!"

"Yes." A great bitterness welled up within him, broke forth in a surge of self-reproach. "June, why did I arrest him! Why didn't I let him escape from that cabin! I took him from you knowin' he loved you, knowin' that you—that you—"

"Loved him?"

Bob's voice was a whisper. "Yes."

He realized suddenly that the violet eyes were very close to him and that one slim young arm had slipped beneath the pillow to circle his neck. It startled him; the look on her face sent a sudden joyous surge of blood through his weakened body. He wondered if he had sunk back into unconsciousness, and if this were some delectable dream. Then her face was pressed against his and she was whispering:

"But I didn't! I didn't love him! I wanted to help him, to encourage him, for your sake."

"For my sake! Then—then you—!"

"Oh, Bob, are *you* blind too? Must I go on confessing to—to every one?"

He knew then that he wasn't dreaming. One arm was strapped to his side, but with the other he drew her to him. From the room beyond came the twang of the guitar and Joe's voice raised in song:

> *"Lock' een the sta-a-able weeth the shi-i-ip,*
> *I'm knock me dow-w-wn from go to sli-i-ip."*

Bob thought it the sweetest song he had ever heard.